VICTORIA ASHLEY

SLADE

WALK OF SHAME #1

SLADE
Copyright © 2014 Victoria Ashley
All rights reserved.

Cover by CT Cover Creations
Stock photo ©123RF.com
Edited by Charisse Spiers
Formatting and Interior Design by Christine Borgford of Perfectly Publishable

CHAPTER ONE

Slade

IT'S DARK.

I love it with the lights off. She insisted on teasing me this way. My arms are tied behind me, my naked body bound to a chair. Goose bumps prickle my flesh as she softly blows on my hard cock, almost breaking my willpower. Her lips are so close, yet not close enough. I insist on teasing *her* this way.

"Na ah, not yet, baby."

She tilts her head up, her blond hair cascading over her shoulders as her eyes lock with mine. They're intense, desperate. She's silently begging me with her eyes, asking me to let her touch me already. I'm used to this. She needs to learn that when you're in my house we play by my rules. "Slade," she whimpers. "Come on already."

"Look down, baby." She tilts her head back down and runs her tongue over her lips as she eagerly looks at my cock;

no doubt imagining what it tastes like in her mouth. "That's it. Don't move."

I lift my hips, bringing the tip of my head to brush her lips. "You want me in your mouth?"

She nods her head and lets out a sound between a moan and a growl. Damn, it's such a turn on.

"How bad do you want it? I want to fucking hear it?"

Her nails dig into my thighs as she growls in aggravation. "More than anything. I want it so just give it to me, dammit. You already know how bad I want it."

A deep laugh rumbles in my throat as she scratches her nails down my legs in an attempt to hurt me. What she doesn't realize is that I welcome the pain. I get off on it.

"Is that all you got, pussycat?" I tease. "If you want my cock, you're going to have to do better than that."

She looks angry now; determined. Standing up, she points a finger in my chest. "You're the one tied up. This is supposed to be my game. Why do *you* have to torture me and make me wait?"

Biting my bottom lip, I nod for her to move closer to me. When she gets close to my face, I slide my tongue out and run it over her lips, causing her to tremble as I taste her. "Show. Me. How. Much. You. Want. Me."

Straddling me, she screams and slaps me hard across the face before yanking my head back by my hair. If I could get any harder, I would.

Fuck me.

"Now, that's what I'm talking about." I press my stiff cock against her ass, showing her just how turned on I am. Then I look her in the eye. "Show me what you can do with your mouth. First impression is always the most important."

A mischievous smile spreads across her face as she slithers her way off my lap and down between my legs. Gripping my thighs in her hands, she runs her tongue over the tip of my dick before suctioning it into her mouth. It hits the back of her throat, causing her to gag. She doesn't care; completely uninhibited. She just shoves it deeper.

Fuck yeah.

I moan as she swirls her tongue around my shaft while sucking at the same time. It feels fucking fantastic. "I told you it's worth the wait, baby. Just wait until I get inside you. It feels better than it tastes."

She pulls back and licks her lips. "Then why don't you show me. My pussy has never been so wet." She stands up and bends over in front of me, exposing her wet lips. I can see the moisture glistening from here; beckoning to suck me inside. She smiles as she runs her fingers over the folds as if she's teasing me; testing me. "You like that?" she asks seductively, tantalizing me. "You want this tight little pussy all for yourself, you greedy little bastard?"

I nod, playing into her little game. She seems to think she's in charge.

"Well, come and get it." She inserts her fingers into her mouth and sucks them clean, before shoving them into her entrance, fucking me with her eyes. Her ass moves up and down in perfect rhythm as she purrs. "I'm waiting." She shoves her fingers deeper. "I want to see those muscles flexing as you ram into me. I want you to . . ."

Well you won't be waiting for long.

Breaking free from my restraints, I stand up, grab her hips and flip her around before slamming her back up against the wall. "What were you saying, baby?" I growl into her ear.

5

I grip both of her ass cheeks and lift her as she wraps her legs around my waist, squeezing. "I'm not sure you can handle what I have to offer." I grip her face in my hand before leaning in and biting her bottom lip, roughly tugging. "You're finally about to get what you've wanted. I just hope you don't have shit to do for the next few days because this might get a little rough. Last time to make your escape, because once I start there's no stopping until you're screaming my name loud; so loud it fucking hurts my ears." I search her eyes waiting to see if she's changed her mind; nothing but raw heat and lust. She still wants it. She's brave. No girl walks into my bed and walks out unscathed. So, she'll get it. I lift an eyebrow. "Okay, then."

I take wide strides across the room to my king-sized bed and toss her atop the mattress. Before she can blink, I am between her thighs, spreading them wide for me. I run my tongue up her smooth flesh, stopping at intersection of her thighs and clean shaven pussy. "You ready for me to make you come without even touching you?"

I begin blowing my cool breath across her swollen, wet pussy. She thrusts her hips up; no doubt her hungry little pussy wanting more and just as I'm about to show her my skills, there's a knock at the damn door.

Bad fucking timing.

Gritting my teeth, I shake my head and look toward the door. "Give me a sec." I step down from the bed and motion for Lex to cover up. When she's done, I call for Cale to come in. "Okay, man."

The door opens right as I'm reaching for my pack of cigarettes and switching the light on. My dick is still standing at full alert, but I could care less. This shit head interrupted my night. If he doesn't like seeing my dick hard, then he should have known better than to come up to my room in the middle of the night.

Stepping into my room, Cale takes notice of my hard on and quickly reaches for the nearest item of clothing and tosses it on my dick. I look down to see a shirt hanging from it. I shake it off. "A little warning next time, mother fucker. I'm tired of witnessing that shit."

Lighting my cigarette, I laugh and take a drag. "Jealous, prick?"

Ignoring me, he walks past me when he sets eyes on Lex. She's been coming to the club for a while now and she's sexy as hell. All of the guys have been trying to get with her, but she's wanted nothing but my cock this whole time. He raises his eyebrows and slides onto the foot of my bed. "Damn, Lex. You get sexier every time I see you."

Gripping the sheet tighter against her body, Lex growls and kicks Cale off the bed. "Go fuck off, Cale. I don't want your dick."

Jumping up with a quickness, Cale reaches for my jeans and tosses them to me. "I don't want to fuck you, Lex. I want to pleasure you. This dick is special." He nods toward me. "Unlike Slade's."

"Fuck you, Cale. What the hell do you want?"

He turns to me after smirking at Lex. "The club just called. We gotta go."

"It's not my night to work, man. Isn't Hemy working?" I take a long drag of my cigarette, letting the harsh smoke fill my lungs as I close my eyes. I really need to release this tension. I will fuck her in front of him if I have to. It wouldn't be the first time I've fucked in front of an audience. "I'm a little busy right now." I dangle Lex's thong from my finger. "If you can't tell."

Not getting where I'm going with this, Cale pulls out his phone and starts typing something in it. "We need to go now. There's a bachelorette party and the chicks asked for us specifically. You know what that means. Plus, Hemy is getting eaten alive right now."

Oh shit. I didn't think it was possible, but my cock just got even harder.

"Well, then I guess we better get started." I put out the cigarette, push past Cale and slide under the sheet. I reach for the condom on the nightstand and rip the wrapper open with my teeth. "This is going to have to be a quick one," I mumble before spitting the wrapper out and rolling the condom over my erection.

Lex looks at me questionably and nods to Cale. "You're going to have sex with me while he watches?"

I smirk as I flip her over and shove her head down into the mattress. "If he doesn't get out of my room, then yes, I'm going to fuck you while he watches." I peek over my shoulder at Cale and he lifts an eyebrow, his interest now peaked. "You've got three seconds and the counting started two seconds ago."

Pointing to Lex, he starts walking backwards while chewing his bottom lip. "As much as I'd love to watch you get fucked, I'm out. This dude gets too wild and I'll probably hurt myself just watching." Picking my wallet up from my dresser, he tosses it at my head, but misses. "Hurry your ass up. I'm changing my shit right now and then we need to go."

Lex moans from below me as I grip her hips, pull her to me and slide inside her. She's extra wet for me, making it easy to give her a good quick fuck. "You're so fucking wet. You were craving this cock weren't you?"

"Dude," Cale complains from a distance; although, I can still feel his eyes watching us.

"Your three seconds were up." I thrust my hips, gripping her hair in both my hands. "Mmm . . . fuck." *Damn that feels good.* "I'll be out in a minute."

"Leave, Cale!" Lex moans while gripping the sheet. "Oh shit! You feel even better than what I've been told. So thick and oh shit . . . it's so deep."

"Damn, that's hot."

"Out!" Lex screams.

"I'm out. I'm out." Cale backs his way out, shutting the door behind him. The truth is, if it weren't for Lex kicking him out, I could've cared less if he stayed and watched. I'm not ashamed.

Knowing I don't have a lot of time, I need to get this chick off fast. That's my rules and I don't have many. She gets off, then I get off. There is no stopping in between for me. Once I start, this is a done deal.

I can feel her wetness thickening. "You've gotten wetter. You like him watching, huh?" I yank her head back and run my tongue over her neck before whispering, "I would've let him stay; let him watch me as I fuck your wet pussy. Does that turn you on?"

Before she can say anything else, I push her head back down into the mattress and slam into her while rubbing my thumb over her swollen clit.

Her hands grip the sheets as she screams out and bites down on her arm, trying to silence her orgasm.

Slapping her ass, I ball my fist in her hair and gently pull it back so her back is pressed against my chest. "Don't hold it back. I want to fucking hear it. Got it?" She shakes her head so I thrust into her as deep as I can go. "Show me how it feels."

Screaming, she reaches back and grabs my hair, yanking it to the side. This makes me fuck her even harder. "Oh yes! Oh God! Slade, don't stop."

Reaching around, I grab her breast in one hand squeezing roughly and bite into her shoulder, rubbing my finger of the opposite hand faster over her slick clit. Her body starts to tremble beneath me as she clamps down hard on my cock. "Oh, shit. Stop, I can't take it. It feels so good, Slade."

I grip her hips and brush my lips over her ear. "You want me to stop?" I pull out slowly, teasing her. "You don't want this cock filling your pussy?" I shove it back in, causing her head to bang into the wall. "Huh, do you want me to stop?"

She shakes her head. "No, don't stop. Shit, don't stop!"

"That's what I thought." I push her completely flat on her stomach, holding my body weight with one arm as I grip the back of her neck and fuck her with all my strength. I want her to remember this because it's the only time she'll be getting my cock and we both know it. It's how I work.

She's squirming below me, shaking as if she's in the middle of another orgasm. "Slade! Oh shit!"

A few thrusts later and I'm ready to blow my load. Pulling out, I bite her ass and stroke my cock as I come.

The relief gives me a high; a fucking drug that I can't get enough of. Nothing else makes me feel this way. Actually, nothing else makes me feel. This is it for me.

My own personal hell.

CHAPTER TWO

Slade

CLOSING MY EYES, I TILT back my second shot of Whiskey. *That's it*, I think, moaning as it leaves a raw, burning sensation in the back of my throat. It's what I need; what I crave.

After rushing Lex out of my room and listening to Cale ramble on about one of his old friends crashing with us for the next week, I need this damn rush; the alcohol pumping through my veins, weakening my demons. Hell, I might even go for another one just for the numbness.

Fuck it. Why not.

Holding up my empty shot glass, I nod at Sarah to come my way. She instantly drops what she's doing to come to me. "Give me another one."

Snatching my empty glass away, she smiles and nods over to Cale and Hemy working their shit on the girls in the back corner. "Shouldn't you be over there showing them how it's done?" She laughs while pulling out a bottle of Jack and filling a new shot glass. "They're both looking a little tired and worn down. You know how bachelorette's are; last night of freedom and all."

I turn around in my stool and look at the two idiots. Cale is standing on a couch grinding his cock in some girl's face while wiping sweat from his forehead. Hemy has some girl on the floor, rolling his body above hers, but he's moving in a rhythm slower than the music.

Tired? How the hell can they . . .

"Yeah, well give me another shot and then I'll show them what's up."

"I'm sure you will, Slade. Keep slamming these back and I might be showing you what's up later." She pushes the shot of Whiskey across the bar and I grab it. "Go ahead. Drink up." She winks.

Smirking, I hold the glass to my lips. She already knows how I work. "We've already had our night, Sarah." I tilt the glass back and run my tongue over my lips, slowly, just to remind her of how I pleasured her. This causes her to swallow hard and her breathing to pick up. "It was hot as fuck too." I slide the glass forward and stand up. "But it goes against my rules."

Her eyes linger down to the very noticeable bulge in my jeans. She smiles while running her finger over the empty glass. "Good to know I can at least still get you hard."

I toss down a twenty and start backing away. "Baby, you get every man hard." I point to the awkward looking guy that has been staring at her since I sat at the bar. "Especially that dude."

She glances at the scrawny dude with glasses and forces a smile. He smiles back and leans over the bar, awaiting conversation. "I so hate you, Slade," she growls and I love it. Growling turns me on.

"That's all right. I'm used to it."

She tosses a straw at me and I knock it away with my hand before turning around and making my way over to the bachelorette party.

The girls are tossing back drinks; some of them standing on tables while a few of them are watching from afar. Those are usually the married ones; the good girls. That's all right though, because I don't need to touch them to pleasure them. They'll still get off.

As I'm about to show my boys up, to my right, I notice two girls dancing and minding their own business. Instantly, my focus goes to the curvy body that is swaying back and forth, drawing my cock to instant attention. It's so seductive it makes my cock hurt.

Skin tight blue jeans mold to her every curve, making me imagine what it would be like to run my tongue over that tight little ass; to taste every inch of her.

Letting my dick do the talking, I walk up to the dance floor, grab the drink out of her hand and set it down on the table beside me.

She looks pissed off, but that's all right. Pissed is sexy as hell on her. It makes me want her more. Her eyes stray from the table I just set her glass on and land on my stomach. Then my chest. Then, slowly, up to my face. She swallows and a look of lust flashes in her eyes. She wants me and I haven't even done anything yet.

Holy fuck. She is beautiful.

My eyes trail from her long blond hair that stops just below her breasts up to her red pouty lips. Damn, I want to suck those between my lips. She's looking at me through long, thick lashes and even in the dimmed lighting; I can see that she has two different colored eyes. I can't make out the colors, but I can see the shade difference.

So fucking hot.

"Umm . . ." She smiles and runs her hand through her hair. "Can I help you with something? We kind of have a private party going on here."

Taking a step closer, I lean in and brush my lips over her ear. "Yeah, I can help you with something," I whisper. "I can help you with a lot of things."

Her breathing picks up and I already know that I have her. It's that simple. "I'm sorry, but I don't even know you." She takes a step back, but her eyes trail down my body before coming back up to meet my face. She looks nervous. I love that. I can teach her a few things. "And I was drinking that."

I watch her with a smirk as she reaches for her drink and pretends to give me a dirty glare. It's not working on me though. I already know her body language and she's already let it slip that I do something to her. "I can give you something better than that."

Her tiny nostrils flare as her eyes rake back down my body, stopping on my fucking crotch. If that's what she wants then I'll give it to her. "Sorry, but I'm not interested. I'm just here for a friend's party."

She likes games. Good thing, because I like them too.

Closing the distance between our bodies, I cup her cheek in my hand. I bring my lips close to hers while looking her in the eyes. Her breath hitches as I press my body against hers and bring my eyes down to meet her lips. "Are you sure about that?"

Her lips begin to move as if she's about to respond and I have the sudden urge to suck them into my mouth; to own them. She's breathing heavy and I can feel the heat radiating from between her thighs that are pressed against my leg while I rub my thumb over her cheekbone.

I feel myself leaning closer until my bottom lip brushes hers. "You're fucking beautiful."

She takes in a quick burst of air and takes a step back. "Umm . . ."

"Slade!" A drunken female shrieks from behind me.

Shit. I hate shriekers.

Exhaling, I turn my head, but keep my eyes glued to the beautiful blond in front of me. For some reason, I don't want to take my eyes away.

Those lips. Fuck me, I want to fuck them. I want them wrapped around my cock.

"About time you got here." A dark haired woman with huge fake tits bounces in front of me and grabs my hand, pulling me away from the beauty in front of me. I see blondie's eyes glance down at my hand, but she quickly turns her head away and clears her throat as if embarrassed. "My favorite piece of eye candy is here." She throws her arms up and starts screaming while pulling me away. "Look everyone. It's fucking, Slade," she slurs.

Smiling to blondie as she watches me, I mouth, "You're mine later."

Her lips part and I can tell she just swallowed. I have her thinking about it. It's written all over her face. Her friend starts nudging her in the side until finally she pulls her eyes away from me and smiles nervously at her friend.

Shit, I've gotta have her. I won't stop until I do.

Spinning on my heel, I pick the brunette up by her hips and sit her down on the chair in front of us. She spreads wide for me and presses her hands against my chest as I step between her legs and slowly grind my hips to the music.

Placing one hand behind my head, I grip her neck with my other as I close the space between our bodies, grinding my hips in a slow, seductive movement as if I'm slowly fucking her.

She moans from beneath me as I let her hands explore my chest and abs. The women here like to touch and I like to give them what they want. It's my job to please them and I'm damn good at it.

"Take it off!" A few girls start screaming.

"Let us see your body. Come on!"

Absofuckinglutely.

Pulling the brunette's chin up, I look her in the eyes as I slowly pull my shirt over my head and toss it down beside me. Most women love it when I make them feel like I'm stripping just for them. It makes them feel special.

She bites her bottom lip as her hands go straight for the muscles leading down to my cock. The girls can never get enough of it; of both.

As much as I'm enjoying getting these women off, there's one woman in particular I want to get off and I'll be damned if I'm going to let her leave here unsatisfied.

CHAPTER THREE

Aspen

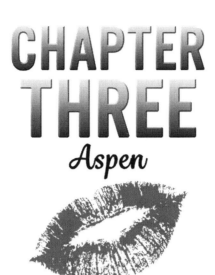

KAYLA KEEPS NUDGING ME TO get my attention, but for some reason I can't seem to drag my eyes away from the jerk-off that is practically dry humping some girl in the corner. She loves it too; over there moaning and rubbing her hands all over his body as if she's about to have an orgasm. How gross. Have some damn class. We aren't in the middle of a damn porn.

A stripper? I shake my head and snort. *A sexy as hell one too. Who the hell does he think he is getting that close to me?*

The bad part of it is, I think he may just be the sexiest man I have ever laid eyes on. Messy black hair that falls over his deep blue eyes and the perfect five o'clock shadow that surrounds a set of full lips. I can't forget that body of pure muscle that you could easily see through that firm fitting white T-shirt he had on. Now, it's off and . . . *crap.* He has me so worked up, I can barely breathe. *This is embarrassing.*

Our lips were so close I could almost taste him. I imagine he probably tastes minty and fresh; perfectly refreshing. For some stupid reason, I had the urge to run my tongue over those full lips. They just looked so soft and inviting; calling me to feel them, suck them. The way he was looking at me; holy shit, it was like he was tasting me in a way I have never been tasted. I liked it. Dammit, why did I like it?

"Um . . . Aspen. Hello. Am I talking to my damn self? Snap out of it."

I suck in a deep breath and pull my eyes away from Mr. Sex himself. "What? I'm listening." I bring my eyes up to meet hers, but they quickly stray back over to *him* as I pretend to pay attention to her.

Brushing her burgundy locks over her shoulder, she rolls her eyes at me and grabs my hand. "Come on. Let's just get closer so you can drool over sexy stripper boy up close. There's nothing to be ashamed of. Stop being so shy. We're here to have fun."

I huff and pull my hand out of her grip. There's no way I'm going over there and giving him the pleasure of seeing me watching him. I'm only here because Paige is getting married. Hell, I'm not even watching *Cale* and I've known him for years. I'll just stay where I'm at. No thank you.

"I'm good, Kayla. I'm not getting in the middle of that orgasm fest. It's pathetic." I hold my drink up and grin. "This is all the pleasure I need while I'm here. Simple as that." I take a huge gulp as my eyes once again land on him and *oh God, that ass*.

His jeans are now hanging half way down his ass, showing his muscular butt cheeks through his white boxer

18

briefs. The busty woman in front of him is desperately tugging on the front of his jeans, working on pulling them down his body. I don't blame her. I want to take them off with my teeth.

Crap, my mind is in the gutter.

Placing his hands behind her head, he pulls her face down by his crotch as he starts grinding his hips up and down in perfect rhythm to the song playing. It's a slow, seductive song that makes me think about sex. Yup, I'm definitely thinking about sex now.

Just as I think he's about to actually let this woman publicly suck his dick or something, he grips her by the hips and pulls her up to her feet. Slowly, he makes his way behind her and his eyes land on me and they stay there, locked with mine.

What the . . . why? Stop looking at me.

I tug on the collar of my white blouse and without meaning to I start fanning myself off. He smiles at this, knowing exactly what he's doing to me. He's doing this on purpose.

Cocky jerk.

Bending the girl over, he grips her hair in one hand and pulls her neck back while grinding his hips on her ass. His eyes bore into mine as he shakes himself out of his jeans and lets all of his sexiness consume us. Yes, he is damn sexy and he knows it. That just pisses me off more. His legs are thick and muscular; covered with random tattoos and every muscle in his body is well sculpted.

Now that he's facing me it's easy to see his defined chest and abs flexing as he moves with the music. The muscles leading down to his briefs are staring at me, flexing with each sway of his hips; calling out to be touched and licked. *Mmm yes. I want a taste . . .*

Holy hell, he's in shape; like a fitness model. Plus, he has random tattoos inked across his chest, sides, lower stomach and arms as well. Hell, he has tattoos all over and it makes him even hotter. They glisten as the perspiration forms on his skin.

He's staring at me, while practically having sex with this girl with his clothes on. Still, I'm standing here watching as if it were me.

What is wrong with me?

I feel myself start to sweat and get a tingling sensation between my thighs as he bites his bottom lip and starts thrusting hard and deep while his eyes devour me. Well, at least I imagine it would be really deep. I can't deny that I bet it would feel so good.

He must notice me sweating because he laughs a little and steps away from the girl that is still bent over with her ass in the air. Ignoring all the girls screaming for him, he starts walking with meaning; unstoppable. With each step, he gets closer and closer to me.

My body is shaking just from his presence and my breathing picks up. I hate my body right now.

His eyes are intense; telling me he wants me as his. A part of me almost wants to give in just from that look alone.

My eyes slowly leave his eyes, searching my way down his muscular body and landing right on his hard dick.

Oh. My. God.

You can see everything through his tight briefs. The thickness of his dick and even the shape of its head. The whole package. He's so . . . hard.

Stopping in front of me, he smirks and tilts his head down toward his cock. My eyes are betraying me. *Damn bastards.* They won't move away. "You know, it's against the rules, but I would let you touch it if you wanted to."

Shaking my head, I pull my eyes away and slam back the rest of my drink. This is my third one and I'm a lightweight; probably not a good thing. I take a step back as he takes a step closer. Clearing my throat, I ask, "Touch what?"

Reaching out, he grabs my hand and places it on the V of muscles that lead down to his briefs, slowly sliding it down his sweaty, slick body. "My cock," he whispers.

My body clenches from his words and I hate it. Yanking my hand away, I grab Kayla by the arm and slam my empty glass down onto the table beside me. I need to get out of here. "Thanks for the offer, playboy, but I'm here to meet a friend and like I said, I'm not interested."

Smirking, he takes a step back as Cale slaps him on the shoulder. "Dude, back away from our temporary roommate. You're freaking Aspen the fuck out, Sir Dick a lot."

I see the smile in his eyes as if he's got me right where he wants me now and he looks like a man that always gets what he wants. Running his tongue over his bottom lip, he backs away slowly, keeping his eyes on me the whole time, until disappearing back into his crowd of fan girls.

Cale gives me a quick hug and apologizes. "Sorry about him. Just ignore him and you'll be fine." He starts backing away and smiles. "We'll catch up later, I promise."

"All right, pretty boy," I call out. "Better hurry and get back to your crazy fan girls."

Cale is the definition of pretty. Short blond hair, striking green eyes and the sweetest dimpled smile you'll ever see. I will never understand why my sister has never hooked up with him.

Turning to Kayla, I let out a deep breath and instantly turn red with embarrassment as she starts laughing. "What!" I yell.

She smirks and pretends like she's giving a blowjob.

"Stop that! You dirty, bitch." I push her shoulder and she laughs. "I need another drink."

She turns toward Slade, dancing his dick off in the middle of some girls. "I would need a drink after that too. Holy shit! That is one fine piece of ass." She starts pulling me towards the bar. "Plus, you need to get your mind off a certain someone," she says to remind me. "Relax a little."

"Yeah," I breathe. "Probably so. I'm not going to let it bring me down this week."

When we reach the bar, the pretty bartender smiles at me and shakes her head.

Wondering if she's laughing at me for some reason, I take a seat on the stool in front of me and give her a hard look. Slade has me all kinds of feisty at the moment and I can't believe he's Cale's roommate. Not good. "What?" I narrow my eyes at her as she reaches for an empty glass.

Scooping up some ice, she looks over my shoulder and laughs again. "Honey, no one turns Slade down. Are you insane? That is one piece of ass that you don't want to miss out on. Trust me."

Trying my best not to look behind me, I fail. I should kick my own ass. I glance over my shoulder to see Slade staring at me while using his shirt to wipe the sweat off his chest. He slowly moves it down his body as if teasing me.

Crap! He even looks sexy doing that.

I growl under my breath and ignore what she just said. Obviously, he's a man whore. "Just give me another drink, please. Make it strong."

The bartender tilts her head and goes about her business. Thank goodness because I really don't want to think about that half naked, sexy asshole anymore.

"Right on," Kayla says happily. "It's a good thing I'm driving your ass around."

"Probably a very good thing right now," I say softly, trying to get my thoughts in check.

After setting eyes on the sexiest asshole I have ever seen, I have a feeling I'm going to need help if I'm going to be in the same house with *him* for the next week.

Crap, I'm in for a ride.

CHAPTER FOUR
Slade

MY NIGHT WAS MADE WHEN Cale said those three little fucking words. *Our temporary roommate*. Apparently, she lives in Rockford and is planning to stay here in Chicago as a bit of a break from home. He wouldn't tell me why and I could care less. It's none of my business. I don't mind sharing my bed; although, Cale will probably offer his to be nice.

That damn pussy.

The look on Aspen's face when she realized she'll be spending the next week in the same house as me was fucking priceless; a dead giveaway that she finds me tempting.

Damn, my cock is hard.

Pushing my cock down, I adjust my jeans and moan.

"Dude, what the shit!" Cale looks over from the driver side and scowls. "Don't tell me you're thinking about fucking her."

Playing stupid, I cross my hands behind my head and laugh. Of course, I'm thinking about fucking her. "Who?"

Cale lets out a long huff and pulls into the driveway. "Fucking, Aspen, you dipshit. She doesn't need you messing with her right now."

I push the car door open and step out before slamming it behind me. When Cale catches up to me, I laugh and lean against the door as a little red Chrysler Sebring pulls up behind my truck. Since I've had a few shots, I made Cale drive us home. I never drive after I've had a few drinks. One of my small list of rules, I never break. They were created for my own good.

"Every girl needs me messing with her; especially that one."

I nod toward Aspen as she steps out of the car looking like a fucking Victoria's Secret model. The sexy, curvy kind that you want to run your tongue over every inch of flesh and savor the fucking taste. You don't just want this woman for dessert. You want her for breakfast, lunch, and dinner too. Any average guy would. Good thing I'm not your average guy.

OH HELL. WOULD SOMEONE PLEASE make him stop looking at me like that? He stares at me; burning his eyes into my body, like he's about to rip my clothes off and pound me against a wall somewhere. It's so distracting.

Don't let him get to you. Don't let him get to you.

25

Taking a deep breath, I close the car door behind me, wave to Kayla and start walking to the porch of Cale's two bedroom home. I've been here before as a guest, but it was back before Cale had a roommate. I have known Cale for years because he and my sister were best friends growing up. He's a good guy and I love him like a brother. I was excited to come here, but now . . . I'm not so sure.

Before I can even step onto the porch, I can see Slade's eyes burning into mine. Hell, I can almost feel them. They're so dark and broody. Is everything about this guy so intense?

I bet sex is.

Mentally slapping myself, I shake off the thought and walk over to Cale. He wraps his arms around me and squeezes me in his usual hug. "Oh man. I've missed you," I say. "Thanks for letting me crash here. You have no idea how much you are helping me out."

Shaking me roughly, he lets go and kisses my forehead. "I missed you too, gorgeous. My house is yours whenever you need it. No need to even ask. You know that."

When I turn back to Slade his eyes look me up and down, branding me into the portals of his memory. He's undressing me with his eyes like he's formulating a plan of attack in his mind; the ultimate predator. I feel it; everywhere. He knows it too. He's a pro at this game.

Now that we're in the lighting of the porch, I can see a scar on his right cheekbone. He catches me staring and lets out a little growl before turning and opening the door to let us in.

I follow behind Cale, in a hurry to get this night over with. I'm so tired I can barely keep my eyes open. I want to ask where I'm sleeping, but I'm afraid Slade might have too much fun with that.

I take a glance around the house to see it looks exactly the same as before: Black furniture, black curtains, sixty inch TV with a huge surround sound. Pretty much everything manly. This place really needs a woman's touch; just not mine.

"So . . ." I lift my eyebrows at Cale, hoping he gets the hint as Slade walks into the kitchen. He doesn't. He just looks at me and raises his eyebrows back in question. One of the things I've learned about Cale is he never gets the hint, ever.

"What do you want to do now?" As the words leave Cale's lips, he then glares over at Slade as he walks back into the living room, shirtless, with a bottle of Whiskey pressed to his lips. "Oh boy."

Slade pulls the bottle away from his mouth and smiles a devilishly sexy smile that makes me wet. "You don't need to ask her that. She wants to come up to my room so I can bend her over my desk and fuck her."

I wrinkle my forehead in shock and anger at him being so outspoken and straight forward.

Seriously!

Taking the only thing I can think of in my outburst of anger, I toss my phone at his head; better that than my favorite heels. He dodges just in time and leans against the couch. The muscles in his arms and stomach flex as he holds the bottle up and takes another swig. "You're a real piece of work. Do you know that?"

"So I've been told," he says stiffly. "You haven't seen anything yet. The next time you're ready to inflict pain, you better be ready to follow through. I'll show you what a real fucking piece of work I am, then."

"You asshole! I will . . ." Bending over, I reach for my high heel and almost fall over. Cale reaches for my arm and steadies me. We'll see what he says when I stab him with my stiletto.

"Whoa, whoa." He turns to Slade and gives him the nastiest look I've ever seen on Cale's pretty face. "Dude, I told you to leave her alone. If she kicks your ass, that's on you. Then, I'll kick your ass just for pissing her off."

I feel my nostrils flare in anger as I find myself checking out Slade's sexy body. His faded jeans are fitted and hanging low on his slender waist. I swear I could kill him just for being so sexy. *That asshole.*

"All right. Your loss, Pen."

Without glancing back, he heads for the stairs and I watch in utter shock as he holds my phone up, smiles and tosses it to me. "You're going to make hating you easy," I growl. "And don't call me Pen, man whore."

"I've heard worse," he says calmly. "Oh and I texted your friend Kayla and asked her to join me tonight."

That prick!

Pulling my eyes from his muscular back, I turn to Cale and growl. Yes, I growled. I am so pissed, I could scream at poor Cale.

"I'm sorry. I'll get his ass in check by the morning." Leading me toward the back of the house, he rubs my shoulders and kisses the top of my head. "You can take my room. I cleaned the sheets for you last night. I'll sleep on the couch so you don't get mauled like a bear in your sleep."

SLADE

Thankful, I exhale and give his muscular frame a hug. I would kiss him if it wouldn't be so weird. "Thanks. I appreciate that. I hope there's a lock on the door now." I look at him with a raised eyebrow, remembering the image of me walking in on him getting sucked off by some girl once. That was awkward.

Laughing, he pushes me into the room and starts closing the door as he takes a step back. "Don't worry, he won't come into my room. He's just being an ass because he's used to all the girls wanting him. I'll keep my eye on him." He rubs his chest and yawns. "I'm crashing."

"Goodnight," I mumble.

As soon as Cale is out of the room, I clutch my phone in my hand and scroll through my text messages. I take a deep breath and exhale when I see that he was lying about texting Kayla. For some reason that pissed me off. The thought of him having sex with her is not something I want to picture.

I strip down to my panties and bra and make a quick phone call while hopping into Cale's bed.

The phone rings a few times and just when I think it's about to go to voicemail, he picks up.

"Hello," Jay yells into the phone. I can barely hear him over the loud music. My heart sinks just knowing what he's up to.

"Jay, are you busy?" I ask with a sigh.

It takes a second before he answers and all I can make out is a female giggling. "Yeah, Aspen. I'm a little busy right now."

I don't say anything for a few seconds. I just listen to his heavy breathing and the sound of her whispering and then giggling. I feel like puking.

"All right. I just wanted to say goodnight." I grind my jaw, trying my best not to cry.

"Okay, goodnight. I'll try to talk to you tomorrow night. Right now is just bad timing. You should really be sleeping by now."

"Yeah." I sigh. "You're right. I am pretty tired. Talk to you later."

Pulling the phone away from my ear, I hit the end button and curl myself into Cale's nice warm blankets. What I wouldn't give to be wrapped up in someone's arms right now. I make myself sick just for wanting it. I just really need an escape from myself right now.

What a shitty night.

CHAPTER FIVE

Slade

SITTING ON THE EDGE OF my bed, I run my hands over my face and close my eyes. I didn't sleep for shit as usual and I have a headache from hell. I've been sitting here, awake for the last two hours, but I can't seem to bring myself to move from this spot. It's eating at me deep today. The pain; it's fucking killing me. Some days are harder than others and I really need to work to get my shit in check.

I let out a deep breath and slip on a pair of my boxer briefs before making my way down the hallway and downstairs. The house is still dark and I can hear Cale snoring from the couch. I'm not surprised, because I'm always the first one up. Like I said, I'm not much of a sleeper. It's the one thing that comes difficult for me.

After slamming back a glass of water, I slip into the bathroom and close the door behind me. I stand there, staring at my reflection in the small, darkened room. The only light shining through is from the small beam coming from the slightly parted shades. It's just enough lighting to let my eyes fall on the scar across my cheekbone. It's not very big.

Fuck, it should be bigger.

Placing my hands in front of me, I grip the sink and lean over it. I feel my breathing pick up as the emotions swarm through me; awakening the madness that I keep buried deep. I have an urge to put my fist through this mirror to stop the pain, but I won't. My hands are already scarred up enough. Anger and rage only douse the pain, but doesn't stop it.

I get distracted when I hear a noise coming from the hallway and then the bathroom door is pushed open. I slowly tilt my head to the side to see Aspen standing there in only a T-shirt.

Shit. She is damn sexy.

She takes a step back when she notices the look on my face. I would too. I'm a monster. The concern in her eyes makes my heart skip a beat and I have no idea why. She doesn't even know me, but she's looking at me as if I'm transparent; seeing straight through to my damaged soul. I don't like it one bit.

"I'm sorry." She pulls her eyes away from mine and tugs on the hem of her T-shirt, causing my eyes to trail down her legs and my grip on the sink tightens. "I didn't realize anyone was in here. It was dark and the door wasn't shut all the way."

Pushing away from the sink, I get my emotions in check and walk toward the door. If I wasn't feeling like shit, I would hit on her right now and tell her all the things I want to do to that beautiful body. I should, but I can't. I've let my inner thoughts take over and pull me down; remind me of the piece of shit that I really am. I know it, everyone else knows it and I've accepted it.

"It's cool. I was just going to take a shower, but I'll let you have it first." I wait for a response. When she doesn't say anything, I stand and turn, now standing in front of her. I grip onto the top of the doorframe and look her in the eyes. I can't tell which one I like more; the blue one or the deep green one. They're stunning. "It's all yours if you want it."

Her eyes dart down to my chest and she swallows before shaking her head and turning away. "It's fine. I can wait. I was just going to take a quick shower and see if Cale would run me to Kayla's. It's not a big deal. He's still sleeping anyways. I'll just go and let you-"

"I'll take you," I say, stopping her mid-sentence while gripping the doorframe tighter. "I have to go to the club here in a bit anyways. I'm filling in for Sarah behind the bar for a few hours."

She looks a bit surprised and not sure if she wants to take me up on the offer. That bothers me for some reason yet I don't know why. "It's fine. You don't have to. I'll just wait. You were already in here anyways."

Releasing the doorframe, I take a step closer and slowly run my hands down her sides, tracing every curve through the thin material. *Fuck, she feels so good*. My hands stop amidst her hips and I squeeze, pulling her body to press against mine. My cock hardens against her stomach and she sucks in a deep breath, but doesn't pull away. A part of her wants this and the more I look at her, the more I fucking want her; a distraction. Fucked up or not, I can't deny that I *need* this distraction, addiction, necessity or whatever else you may

33

want to call it. I've gotten used to the harsh judgments of my lifestyle.

"We can take a shower together." I brush my lips over her neck and whisper, "I can dirty you with my body and then clean you with my tongue."

She tilts her neck and allows me to run my tongue up it as if that's the pass code to her arousal. She likes it. I can tell by her soft moans. "Have you thought about what my cock will feel like inside you?" I suck in her earlobe and bring my hands down to cup her ass. It's the perfect fit. "I want to fuck you. I want you to know what it feels like to have me deep." I lick my lips and breathe into her ear. "Inside you."

Her chest pushes out as she takes a deep breath. "I don't even know you." She places her hands on my chest and backs away. "Plus, I don't like you. Now, if you don't mind. *One* of us has to take a shower first. You or me? Pick one."

She presses her legs together and I can tell she's trying to hide that I have her pussy aching for my touch. She's wet and ready for me. I don't have to check; I just know. That's okay 'cause my cock wants it just as much.

Enjoying watching her squirm, I smile and lean into the doorframe. "I'm going to take care of that for you."

Her eyes watch mine as I look down at her black panties that are barely peeking out from under what I assume is one of Cale's old shirts. For some reason, the thought of stripping her out of another man's shirt turns me on; gives me a rush knowing I can.

She watches me intently, but doesn't say a word as I grab the bottom of the T-shirt and slowly lift it over her head and toss it behind me. She's standing there in just her thong and bra. Her breasts are plump and firm, squeezed into a tiny black bra to match her panties; her cleavage playing peek-a-boo. My cock instantly strains to break free from the material as I imagine dropping to my knees in front of her and devouring her fucking pussy; the perfect breakfast.

Running my hand up her tight little stomach, I press her up against the wall with my hand above her head. "Touch yourself for me."

She's hesitant at first, but nervously licks her lips as she slides her hand down the front of her panties, her eyes never leaving mine.

"That's it. I bet it feels so fucking good." I press into her with my body as I squeeze her hip. She takes her eyes away from mine, so I grab her chin and pull her face to meet mine. "Don't turn away. Look at me while you touch yourself." I lick my lips in satisfaction as she does what I say. "Does your pussy feel good, baby?"

She nods her head and places her bottom lip between her teeth as she starts moving her hand up and down.

"I bet. Now imagine it were my fingers fucking your tight little pussy and rubbing your swollen clit. So thick and firm, filling you up as I pleasure you." Her hand quickens as she closes her eyes and moans. "That's it. You like the thought of me pleasuring you, don't you? Fuck yourself harder. I want to fucking hear your pussy wet for me."

Her breathing picks up and she begins shaking as if she's about to have an orgasm. She stops abruptly and opens her eyes, staring into mine. "What the hell am I doing?" Pulling her hand out of her panties, she places her hands against the wall behind her and looks down at my hard cock with longing. I can see the want in her eyes, but she's fighting it for some reason. "I'm not doing this. This is beyond messed up."

Grabbing her hand, I lift it and slowly suck her wet fingers into my mouth, tasting her. I suck her fingers clean while looking her directly in the eyes. *Oh fuck.* My cock just got harder. "Damn, baby. You taste so good. I can fucking taste your frustration and need. Why not let me ease that frustration; show you what it's like to have me taste you, suck you, and fuck you."

I smile against her fingers before placing my hand in the back of her hair and pulling her mouth towards mine. Just as I'm about to kiss her, she turns her head away and sidesteps around me. "Don't call me baby and I shouldn't have done that. Now get out so I can take a shower."

She looks away embarrassed as I lick my lips one last time, tasting her on my mouth. Without saying a word, I turn around and walk out of the bathroom.

I could tell by the nervous look on her face that even she can't believe she just did that in front of me. I could also tell by the look in her eyes that she wanted me to stay. She wants me and I'm going to show her it's okay to have me.

TWO HOURS LATER AND HERE I am, leaning against my motorcycle, watching with satisfaction as Aspen exits the house with a look of frustration. She looks so tense and . . . unpleased. Sickly enough, this pleases me.

Judging from her hour long shower, I would say she definitely couldn't please herself without my help. That only gives me more reason to want to please her. To show her how I can make her feel.

Crossing my legs in front of me I smile as she approaches and gives me a look so dirty, I might just need another shower. I don't think she understands what that look does to me. It's so damn sexy. "Did you have a good shower?" Tossing my helmet up, I catch it and hold it out for her to grab. "I would've finished you off; gave you the best orgasm of your life."

"Shut up," she growls. Rolling her eyes she exhales while looking at the helmet in my hand. "Seriously? You want me to get on that? Why not take the truck?"

Since she refuses to take the helmet, I slide it on her head and rev the engine. "Just get on. I don't have all day."

She shakes her head once before throwing her leg over the motorcycle and hopping on behind me. "You think this shit is funny, don't you? What you did back there."

I look over my shoulder at her sullen face and smirk. "What?"

"You know what I'm talking about. Don't play stupid, *Slade*," she growls. "You did that on purpose."

"What did I do? I want to fucking hear it."

She gives me a dirty look and runs her tongue over her teeth in frustration. "Nothing. Nothing at all, okay."

"All right. Then, I apologize for doing nothing at all. Happy?"

She lets out an exasperated huff before grabbing my shoulder with her left hand and placing her other hand behind her, keeping her distance. "Let's just go. Kayla is waiting on me."

"Grab my waist," I say firmly. When she doesn't make a move to grab me, I reach for both of her arms and wrap them around my waist. She stiffens as if she doesn't know what to do. "Keep your arms around me. Got it."

If she's not worried about her safety then she can walk. It's as simple as that.

"Fine. Let's just get this over with." Locking her fingers around my waist, she tilts her head to the left. "Go down to the light and make a left. Then go ten blocks and make a right. All right. Be careful too. I want to actually make it there before she has to go to work."

Swallowing back my remark, I take off causing her to squeeze her arms around me for safety. I smile to myself, feeling the awkwardness in her touch. She definitely needs to loosen up and give into her needs.

After a few minutes of riding in silence her arms finally start to relax and I can feel them inching higher, getting closer to my chest.

Every time I make a turn or pass someone, I can hear a little gasp from her as my muscles tighten from below her hands. She's trying hard to hide it, but I can tell she wants to explore. It gives me a fucking rush.

About five minutes later, we pull up to a little white house to see her friend outside waiting on her. The red car from the other night is sitting in the driveway and it makes me wonder why she didn't just ask her friend to pick her up if she hates me so much.

As soon as I stop the bike, she jumps off and takes my helmet off as fast as her fingers will allow her. She tosses it in my lap and scowls. "Thanks for the ride, jerk."

Smiling at her and her hot little friend, I slide the helmet on my head. "Anytime." I look down toward her pussy. "And thanks for the show." I wink and she looks away embarrassed. I can feel her eyes burning into me as I take off. Hell, I don't mind. She can undress me with her eyes anytime she wants.

WHEN I PULL UP AT the bar, it's completely empty. I toss my cigarette and jump off my motorcycle while looking around, preparing myself. This is a shit shift and you don't make crap at this time. The bar opens at eleven, but really the business doesn't take off until late at night when the entertainment comes in.

I don't mind doing Sarah favors, though, because she has a young child and I want her to be able to be there for him when it's needed. That shit is very important. If anyone else asked me to cover this crap shift, my answer would be hell no.

Now, I'll be stuck here for the next few hours practically talking to myself and hoping for someone to stop in and entertain me. Not my idea of a good day. It gives you too much time to think.

Hilary has already been here and has left. I can tell as soon as I unlock the back door and walk in. The lights are all turned on and the bar is set up and ready to go.

Hilary is the owner. She's an older woman, maybe in her early fifties. She only stops in once a day and usually it's when no one is here. She's good at what she does, though, and helps out whenever she can. I really like her as a person and a manager. She treats us well.

A couple hours into my shift, a woman around my age, mid-twenties, finally comes into the bar and takes a seat in front of me.

I've seen her in here a few times before and I have to admit that I've thought about taking her home. She's a natural redhead with a small freckled nose, full lips and a nice set of breasts. She looks sexy as fuck in those tight little suit skirts. She has to work in some office somewhere. I like the thought of dirtying her. She looks like she needs a good fuck to relieve some of the tension she is carrying around.

Taking a seat in front of me, she smiles and sets her purse down beside her. "I'm taking a quick break from work. Give me a drink of your choice. Anything will do." Her eyes rake over my body as I reach for a glass and come her way. There's a look saying she's looking for what I call the fuck and fly; short and hard. It's more of a business exchange between two people. I'm used to the look; prone to it. "I'm going to cut to the chase, okay. I don't have a lot of time, but I have a little time." She smirks while watching me with desperate eyes.

I'm listening . . .

Reaching for a bottle of Jack, I pour it half way up and add a splash of coke and a little lime juice. It may be a little strong, but she looks like she can handle it. She looks like she can handle a lot of things.

Setting the drink down in front of her, I lean over the bar as she reaches for my shirt and pulls me to her. "I've heard a lot of good things about your *dick*. I need to release some tension and I want you to *fuck* me. Can you do that? Nothing more. I'm a very busy woman."

I let my lips brush over her ear before whispering, "For the things I do, you would need a lot more than just a little time." I place my hand behind her neck and pull her closer to my lips. "I would tie you up to my bed, blindfold you and devour your pussy with my tongue. Then when I was done, I would stand you up against my wall, bind your hands above you and fuck you until you can't walk. I would tease you slowly at first to learn your body and what it wants. Then I would fuck you so hard and thoroughly you will never want another cock. I don't think that is what you're looking for. Trust me, it's not easy moving on to just a quick lay after that."

A throat clears from nearby.

"I see you're still on the prowl, son."

Gritting my teeth, I pull away from the redhead and bring my eyes up to meet the one man I wish I could stay away from: my father. He's more like the devil in a fucking suit. He's standing there as if he's so fucking perfect and can't do any wrong. It pisses me the hell off.

"What are you doing here?" I begin finding things to do; pretending to be busy. The last thing I want to do is deal with him at the moment.

Stepping up to the bar, he fixes his tie and takes a seat. "Do I need to have a reason to come see my son? We haven't spoken in over two months."

Walking over to stand in front of him, I lean down and get in his face. "We both know why too. Don't come in here acting as if it's my fault. Get out of here with that shit."

"Son, calm down." Pulling out his wallet he searches through it. "I'll take a Scotch on the rocks."

Rolling my neck to keep my tongue in check, I make him his drink. I set it down in front of him and lean against the register while watching him sip on it.

He makes a sour face while setting the glass back down. "I see not much has changed since the last time we've talked." I watch him with anger while he adjusts his tie as if he's better than me. "When will you realize this lifestyle isn't going to change anything? It won't make things better."

Gripping the counter, I lean over the register and turn my head away. I can't stand to look at him. "Don't even say it. I don't need to hear this shit. I'm fine with my life. Why don't you get back to yours and stop worrying about mine? Don't fucking judge me."

We both look over as the redhead slams back her drink and stands up. "I'm out, boys." She looks at me and winks. "Maybe another time."

I don't say anything. I just watch as she leaves. I'm glad, because she doesn't need to hear this.

"You don't think I'm concerned about my son? That I don't see that you've thrown your life down the drain? It pisses me off." He takes another sip and then scoots it across the bar. "You're better than this. Just because-"

"Don't you fucking say it," I growl out at him in warning and shake the counter.

"I'm just telling you that there's still meaning in your life and you need to find that again. The pain will never go away. I get that but-"

"Fucking stop! Do you understand me?" My voice comes out firmly. "Don't you say another word about it. It's done. Over. I've moved on."

Looking me in the eyes, he stands up and picks up his glass for me to see. "This is what you call moving on? A career as a bartender that strips on the weekends and has meaningless sex with any tramp you can slip your dick into. No, son. This is not moving on. It's fucking numbing the pain."

Grinding my jaw, I swing my hand across the counter, knocking over the bottle of Scotch along with a bunch of other items like limes, straws, and cocktail napkins. "You just don't know when to stop, do you? This is why we don't talk. This is why I stay away. You won't let me live." Turning to leave, he stops and throws down some money. "No, I'm trying to help you live and stop being a piece of shit. Get your shit together before it's too late. You're twenty six years old for fucks sake. Act like it."

I hear him walking away, but I refuse to look his direction and show him just how worked up I am. He always fucking does this; acts as if he knows what I'm going through or how the fuck I feel and *should* feel. No one does.

Fighting to catch my breath and calm down, I lean over the bar and grip the front of my hair in my hands. I feel like going fucking mad right now. Today is not a good day to think about this shit.

I'm pissed. Pissed at my father and pissed at myself for knowing he's right.

Picking up a bottle of Vodka, I toss it across the room at the wall. It shatters against the wall, leaving the clear liquid dripping on the floor. It doesn't do shit to calm me down though. So, I just stand there and stare at the ceiling.

"Well . . . I see it's extremely busy in here today."

I look over with narrowed eyes to see Aspen walk in. She's no longer wearing her clothes from yesterday. Now, she's wearing a pair of faded jean shorts and a white tank top that shows the pink outline of her bra. She must've had her clothes in Kayla's car. She looks . . . good. This look fits her.

Exhaling, I stand up straight and gesture around me. "Yeah, really busy. I hope you're not here for a drink because I might not be able to handle making you one," I say sarcastically.

She leans against the front of the bar and starts fingering the remaining napkins. "I'm here because Kayla had to go to work and Cale isn't home. I don't have a key to get in and he didn't pick up the phone." She looks down at the mess by my feet and then looks up at me. "I suppose you could use a little company anyways."

"I guess," I mumble. "Doesn't look like I have much of a choice." I reach for a glass and scoop it full of ice. "Want a drink?"

"Just a Sprite will be fine. I only drink when I'm out at parties. It's kind of my thing. I'm a lightweight."

I watch her as she sits down in front of me and chews on her lip. "Are you nervous?" I study her reaction to the question that is making her cheeks turn red.

Shaking her head, she reaches for the glass after I finish filling it and pulls it to her lips. "Why would I be nervous? You think you make me nervous? No. You just make me mad. Those are two different things."

Nodding my head in agreement, I say, "You're not the only one."

I'm used to it. Hell, I'm pissed at myself most of the time.

She laughs under her breath and sticks the tip of the straw into her mouth. "I bet there are a lot of pissed off women running around this world due to you. I just get that vibe."

Challenging her, I lean over the bar and pull the straw out of her mouth with my tongue, being sure to get close to her mouth. "Oh yeah," I whisper. "What kind of *vibe* is it that you get from me?"

Backing away, she watches my mouth as I chew on her straw. She clears her throat and averts her eyes when she sees that I notice her staring. "A bad one," she replies.

I stand up and spit out the straw when I see Cale walk in. "Dude, what are you doing here?" For some reason the thought of him being here to pick Aspen up pisses me off.

"Sarah called and said she won't be able to make it to work at all today because her son's doctor appointment is taking longer than she expected. Figuring you wouldn't want the full shift, I offered to come in until seven."

He walks up behind Aspen, wraps his arms around her and squeezes. "Hey, gorgeous. What are you doing here?"

She places her hands on his arms and smiles. "Hey, pretty boy," she says teasingly. "I couldn't reach you earlier so I had Kayla drop me off here."

Looking up from behind Aspen, Cale gives me a concerned look. "Yeah, so your dad stopped by this morning, but judging from the look of this place he's already been here too," he says looking down at the ground.

"I don't even want to hear it. Thanks for the fucking warning."

Cale releases Aspen and steps behind the bar. "I didn't say shit. He must've figured it out on his own. It's pretty simple to find your ass."

A few guys walk in and take a seat next to Aspen at the bar. I notice the preppy, clean cut one staring at her with a creepy ass smile and I have the urge to shove my fist down his throat.

He better not try to pick her up. She doesn't need a guy like that. She needs one that is going to fuck her good and please her so good that it hurts. He looks like too much of a pussy to handle her.

"Hey," he says to Aspen. "Alex."

Cale starts talking to me, but my attention stays focused on *Alex* to be sure he doesn't sign his fucking death wish.

"Aspen." She shakes his hand and then looks away uncomfortable.

Cale nudges me as he goes to approach the guys. "Get your ass out of here. I got it from here. Hemy will be coming in around four so it's all good."

"Huh," I mumble. I pull my eyes away from Aspen and look up at Cale.

"I got it, man. Aspen can hang out here while I work so she doesn't have to be at the house by herself. I'm sure you have shit to do."

Looking back toward Aspen, I notice the creepy guy has somehow gotten closer. Cale is taking their drink order and he doesn't even notice. Seriously?

"No, man. Aspen is coming with me. I don't have shit to do."

Aspen looks up and watches as I clock out.

"Come on. We're leaving."

She looks at me for a second as if she didn't hear me right.

Grabbing my helmet, I walk around to the other side of the bar and reach for her hand, pulling her up to her feet. "Let's go."

Cale and the creepy dude give me a weird look, but I could care less. I'm not leaving her here with that fucking preppy douche.

Aspen looks like she's about to say something until I look her in the eyes and clench my jaw. Instead, she turns beside her to look at Cale. "I'll see you when you get home."

He gives me a warning look before turning to Aspen. "Don't let this dick get to you. If he does, let me know." He turns back to me and scowls. "And don't worry, asshole. I'll clean up your mess."

Waving him off, I walk her out of the bar. When we get to my bike, I toss her my helmet while straddling my bike. "Get on."

CHAPTER SIX

Aspen

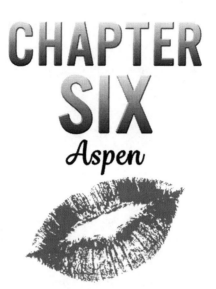

SITTING ON THE BACK OF Slade's motorcycle with my arms wrapped around his waist is the last thing I thought I'd be doing right now. Just earlier I wanted to rip his hair out and choke him, but I have a feeling he might like that type of thing. I might even like doing it to him. That's the sad part.

Since leaving the club, we've been riding for the last hour in dead silence. I have a feeling he needs this at the moment and hell, I do too. It's relaxing having the cool breeze hit against your skin as you ride with no worries; not knowing where you're going or where you'll end up at. The only problem is - it feels like it's about to rain. I can smell it and almost taste it.

Yup, here it comes. Perfect timing.

Holding on tighter, I bring my body closer to his as the rain suddenly hits, pouring off the helmet and soaking my shirt. It's cool. Cooler than I expected, giving me instant chills. My nipples harden as the fabric of my now wet shirt rubs against them. Maybe it wasn't the best idea to go with lace today.

Slade tilts his head up, takes a deep breath and slowly releases it. I can feel his body tensing beneath my arms and I feel myself unintentionally squeeze tighter as he makes a quick right. He rides down a path hidden beneath the trees until finally making a stop in the middle of nowhere.

Grabbing for my hand, he helps me off the bike before he quickly hops off and yanks his gray T-shirt over his head and holds it above me. He slowly backs me up until we're standing below a huge tree, hidden from the rain.

He's standing there soaked, looking at me through long, wet lashes. He has the most amazing blue eyes I have ever seen. I want to pull my gaze away, but I can't. I'm hypnotized. As much as I hate to admit it, he's so damn beautiful; dangerously beautiful. His black hair is wet and slicked back from the rain. It's thick and slightly long. I love that. The focal point is those lips. *Oh God, those lips.* The rain is falling on them, beading, and dripping down. With each drop that falls, it causes him to keep using his tongue to dry them. It's so damn distracting.

"Here. Use this." I pull my eyes away from his lips and take hold of his shirt, holding it above my head. "It's not a damn umbrella, but it will help."

He turns away and walks out into the open, but stops to stand in the pouring rain. I watch as he runs his hands over his face, the rain pouring over his head and arms while soaking his jeans. His bare chest is moving up and down as if he's trying to fight some deep emotions and with each move, his muscles flex, making me very aware of his sex appeal. It's confusing. I don't know if I want to hug him, slap him or fuck him. All I know is that I definitely want to be doing something to him.

After a few minutes of him just standing there, I walk away from the safety of the tree and hold his shirt above both of our heads. By now, it's completely drenched and not serving much of a purpose, but I don't take notice. Someone else has captured my attention. I'm standing on the tip of my toes, trying my best not to lose my balance and fall into him.

It takes him a moment, but he finally turns around. Looking me in the eyes, he reaches for his shirt and throws it down beside him. His eyes are intense; dark. "I need to finish what I started," he growls. He takes a step forward and I take a step back, but his stride is wider than mine. He leans in close to my ear and whispers, "I've been craving your pussy all fuckin' day. That sweet smell from earlier has my mouth watering for another taste."

He doesn't even hesitate before grabbing me by the hips and picking me up. It's as if he already knew I was going to let him do what he wants to me. It angers me, but I have to admit it has me so turned on I don't think I could say no if I tried.

I want to say something; protest or scream no, but I don't. I should, but I won't. I'm too wrapped up in what he's about to do to me. I'm not thinking clearly. My thighs are moistening with every look at his beautiful body and every filthy word that exits his mouth.

He walks toward his black motorcycle with me wrapped around his waist. Just thinking about the way he made me feel this morning without even touching me has me so turned on that I can already feel the ache between my legs just waiting to be released; pulsating to be filled by his dick. It's new to me. It's what *he* does to me.

Setting me down beside his motorcycle, he places one hand on my waist while working the button on my wet shorts with the other. I try to look at his face to see what he's feeling at the moment, but its void of any emotions. He's hard to read and it gives me an adrenaline rush; a need to figure him out.

His hands are working fast to pull my shorts down my legs and lift my feet out of them. Even with them being wet, he is a pro at stripping me out of them. He's good at getting what he wants and it makes me wonder if he's just as good when he gets it.

Standing here almost naked, I feel myself panting as he balls my thong in his hand and yanks. The thin strings rip apart, baring my throbbing pussy to him. My first thought is to cover myself up, but he lifts me up and sets me down so I'm straddling the back of his motorcycle.

I feel my legs spread wider as he runs his hands up my thighs and licks the rain from his full lips. Sitting here right now makes me feel dirty, but a part of me really needs this right now. Maybe letting him pleasure me will be enough to take my mind off things for the moment; not worry about what a certain someone is doing.

"Oh, fuck." He grips my thighs and bites his bottom lip. "The taste of your sweet pussy has been on my tongue all day; teasing me and making my fucking cock hurt. You better hold on tight while I devour your pussy; taste you in ways you've never been tasted."

Gripping my thighs, he pulls me closer to the edge of the motorcycle and runs his tongue up my thigh while grazing my flesh with his teeth. I can already feel myself squirming on the wet bike, trying not to slip off. My heart is going wild in my chest, making it hard to breathe.

Oh. My. Goodness.

"You like that, don't you," he asks against my thigh. "I bet you're already imagining what it's going to feel like when I run my tongue up your wet little pussy." He bites into my thigh and pulls me closer so my legs are over his shoulders. It hurts, but feels so good at the same time. My breathing picks up as he nibbles a little harder. "You like it when it hurts, baby?" He pulls away and lets the rain fall against my swollen clit. It has me wishing his mouth was there instead, to ease my ache.

Just touch me already . . .

An aching pleasure runs throughout my body, causing me to tremble as he inches his way up to my inner thigh, right beside my pussy and bites down onto my skin. I shake my head and squirm out of his reach in an attempt to get away. I can't handle it. It's too much. He feels my pull and yanks me back down by my thighs so I reach out and yank his hair making him look up at me. "Not so rough, asshole. Don't make me regret this anymore than I already do."

"Fuck," he groans out. He closes his eyes and moans. *Oh my, that moan. So deep and rough.* "Pull my hair again and I will fuck you instead of just licking you. Got it?"

Knowing that I'm pushing my luck with him, I release his hair and grip onto the bike handlebars behind my head. I'm already too far to turn back now. I want his tongue, but that's it. Nothing more. This is it. Just one time. Just . . .

"Oh shit," I moan out as his tongue slides up my pussy, slowly and teasingly. "This can only happen once. You know that, right?" I fight to catch my breath. "This is wrong in so many ways."

He looks up from between my thighs with a sly grin. He's a dirty little snake that has me in his grips and he knows it. "Yeah, but it feels so fucking right, doesn't it?"

I don't answer. I don't want to. All I want to do is close my eyes, lean back and let his tongue work its magic to release the tension I've had built up since this morning. When he sucked my wetness into his mouth and tasted me, I almost gave in right there and let him have me. It took every bit of strength to fight my urge to pull him into the shower and let him have his way with me; to take me just once.

His tongue works slowly at first to spread the moisture up my folds. He's being gentle and teasing me, making me want more. His rhythm is precise and in control as if he knows the exact spot to work me up. He's slowly building me up, knowing I'll want more at the end. He's good; a pro. He's in control of his game and it makes me want to knock him down a notch; tease him a little.

I catch myself moaning as he slides his tongue down further and shoves it into my pussy as deep as it will go. He's fucking me with his tongue. The feel and the thought is enough to almost bring me to climax . . . but I fight it. I'm not ready yet and I have a feeling he won't let me get off so easily anyways.

After a few seconds he slips his tongue out and slides it up and over my clit before sucking it into his mouth. It feels so good I have to reach out and grip his hair again. I feel myself pulling and the harder I pull the better his tongue pleases me. He gets off on this and I plan to use this to my advantage.

I yank his hair to the side and he sucks my clit so hard that I scream out in pleasure and almost fall over, but he catches me. I can feel him growling against my clit and it deepens the pleasure and makes me want more as he holds me steady. "Oh shit! Oh shit!"

"Fuck this shit! I want to fuck you so bad and make you scream louder while I'm pounding your tight little pussy. It's so hot hearing me pleasure you." Standing up, he runs his tongue over his lips and places both of his hands on his bike, hovering above me. "You want me to fuck you?" He runs his tongue up my neck and stops at my ear. "Just say the word and I'll end that throbbing ache between your legs. I'll fuck you so good that my cock will be the only one you ever fucking think about again. Let me show you."

I shake my head and place my hand on his chest. "No. Dammit, Slade." I give him a shove, but against his firm body, it doesn't even make him budge. It only makes me want him more. "I don't need you to fuck me and I don't want you to. Just finish what you started, dammit."

Wiping the rain off his face, he spreads my legs wider and places his thumb over my clit and starts rubbing. "Why? Are you afraid it will feel too good? You scared that I might please you better than anyone else can?" I look at him and swallow while trying to pretend his words aren't having the effect on me that they are. "My cock will feel so good in that tight little pussy." Grabbing the back of my head with one hand, he shoves a finger inside me and sucks in his bottom lip. I moan and take a deep breath, feeling the thickness of his finger move in and out, making my body feel hot and tingly. "See how wet I make you."

Closing my eyes, I moan and grip onto his wet hair. I have the urge to pull it and push him even further. I want his finger deeper. I need to get off. "You're an asshole for doing this and you know it," I say between deep breaths.

"Oh yeah, baby,'' he breaths into my ear. "Fucking show me how much of an asshole I am and I'll show you how good I am at pleasing you. You want me to please you; you have to fucking work for it."

What an asshole.

"Fuck you!" I scream as I dig my nails into his back, wanting to hurt him. "You're such an asshole."

He freezes and looks me dead in the eyes, clenching his jaw muscles. His eyes look fierce and I start to wonder if maybe I shouldn't have done that.

"I'm-"

"Don't finish that," he cuts me off.

Without saying another word, he lifts me up off the motorcycle and holds me up high enough for me to squeeze my thighs against his face. I can feel his lips brushing my clit and it already makes me want to lose control.

Oh shit.

Gripping my ass in his hands, he squeezes while his tongue works on catering to the aching throb between my legs. I grab onto his hair as I arch my back and scream. I scream so loud that it hurts. It actually hurts. My heels dig into his back as I continue to hang here while he pleasures me. He doesn't seem like this is straining him at all.

I have never felt anything so good in my life. This is definitely not what I was expecting. I feel the heat surging through my body and I can tell that I'm almost there. I'm so damn close that it hurts. "Shit, it feels so good. Don't stop, Slade. Faster . . ."

He grips me tighter and sucks my clit into his mouth right as my body trembles in his arms and I'm brought to climax by his tongue. *Damn, that magical tongue. I'm so damn ruined.*

"Holy shit, Slade. What did you just do to me?" I suck in a deep breath and release it. My heart is pounding so fast that I'm starting to feel dizzy. "Put me down, dammit. Put me down."

He runs his hands up my legs before grabbing my waist and helping me down to my feet. His eyes bore into mine as I take a step back and reach down for my shorts as fast as I can.

I feel like such an idiot for letting him get me off. I don't even like this guy. He's a jerk; nothing but trouble. The fucking devil in disguise, looking to taint my soul and consume my every thought. *I really need to get out of here.*

He leans against his bike, giving me a cocky look as I quickly slip my shorts on and wipe the water off of my face. "I'm ready to go. Take me back to the house."

Without saying a word, he reaches for his helmet, slips it on my head and jumps onto the bike. I grab his hand as he offers it for help. "What about your shirt?"

"Fuck it. I don't need it." I feel his chest rumble as he laughs under his breath. "What about your panties?"

"Screw you, Slade."

He revs up the engine, makes sure I'm holding on tight and then takes off.

THE RAIN STOPPED ALMOST IMMEDIATELY after we left. The ride back was in total silence. Exactly how I expected it to be. By the time we get back to the house, all I want to do is get as far away from *Slade* as I can. I feel so stupid for letting him work me up the way he did and catch me in a moment of weakness.

All it does is show him that he's right; he gets whatever he wants. I told myself I wouldn't let this happen, that I would be good this week and take some *me* time to figure out my life. So much for that. I feel like such a failure for being so careless.

I quickly hop off the motorcycle and slide the helmet off my head. Slade stays seated and watches me as I hand him the helmet. I can't help but to notice how sexy he looks shirtless on that damn motorcycle. Those tattoos and that damn perfect body. I hate it. No one should be allowed to look that devilishly sexy. "You're not coming in?" He slides the helmet on his head and adjusts the crotch of his jeans.

He turns away, takes a deep breath and reaches into his pocket. "Here's the key. I'll be back tonight."

I reach for the key and swallow. For some reason I don't want him to leave. Yeah, I wanted to get far away from him, but I wanted him to at least be in the house. "All right then," I say aggravated. "And just so you know, that is never happening again. Got it? Stay as far away from me as you can. You got to me in a moment of weakness. It won't happen again."

He grips the handles, clenches his jaw and watches as I walk away. I don't know why he even bothers waiting. I'm sure he's ready to get as far away from me as I am him. That's probably a good thing. The two of us being around each other is nothing but bad news. He's no good for me.

Letting myself in the house, I go straight for Cale's room and fall face first onto his bed. I'm so pissed at myself that I scream like a child. I'm twenty three years old and I still have no control over my life. I need to stay far away from Slade before he makes everything more difficult.

I knew he was going to be trouble from the second I laid eyes on him at the club. I just knew it. Heck, even his name screams trouble. Slade Merrick. Enough said.

CHAPTER SEVEN

Slade

I'VE NEVER HAD A WOMAN act as if *me* pleasing *her* disgusted her. This is a fucking first. I can't say that I like it. As a matter of fact, it pisses me off. She knows damn well that she enjoyed it. I bet she's never had someone make her scream that loud before; make her come on contact. She's just afraid to admit it; afraid to give into her needs; afraid that I'll fuck her too good. That has to be it.

With the way she has me feeling at the moment, the last thing I want to do is go and exist in the same house as her just to have her avoid me and act as if she doesn't want it as much as I do. I'm not down for that shit right now. I need to get some things off my mind; cool off a bit.

Out of habit, I end up at *Walk of Shame*. Pulling my motorcycle in the back parking lot, I yank my helmet off before slamming it down on my seat and shoving my motorcycle. Cale and Hemy better be ready to keep the drinks flowing, because I have a feeling that I will be here for a while.

Stay far away from her. Yeah, I'll fucking stay far away.

I push my way through the back door, walk over to my locker and grab a shirt. I get ready to put it on, but say *fuck it* instead. I'll end up without it on by the end of the night anyways. I toss it down and make my way into the bar.

I notice that the crowd is finally starting to show up. Perfect fucking timing. There should be plenty of entertainment to keep me busy.

As I approach the bar, I see Cale sitting on the edge of the bar talking to a group of women. They all seem to be laughing; fucking entertained.

He nods and jumps off the bar when he sees me. "Dude, why the hell do you look so pissed? I thought you were going to keep Aspen company until I get off?"

Leaning over the bar, I grab for the nearest liquor bottle and reach for an empty glass. "Yeah well, she's not the easiest to entertain. I'm pretty sure she'd rather be alone right now."

Cale tilts his head back with a dirty look as he watches me pour a drink. "Yeah . . . or maybe it's just you she doesn't want to be around."

"Fuck off, Cale. I'm not in the mood today."

"Yeah, well nothing new there."

Slamming back my drink, I set the empty glass down on the bar and take a step closer to Cale so we're face to face. I want to see him when he says it. "What the hell is that supposed to mean?"

Looking away from me, he sighs and takes a step back. "You know what I mean. You're just not the same person you used to be. You're my best friend, but seriously, you need to . . ." He huffs and grips the towel over his shoulder. "Never mind. I've got work to do."

"Yeah. Me too. I have *a lot* of fucking work to do." I pour another drink and make my way over to one of the empty couches. Lucky for me, everyone seems to be in the back room with Hemy so I can get a few minutes to myself.

I set my drink down on the table next to me and lean forward with my head in my hands and my elbows resting on my knees. I just can't get over the fact that I'm so pissed off at this woman. This morning my past consumed my thoughts and now the fact that this woman angers me like nothing else has taken over; has me completely worked up. The bad part is, the more she angers me the more I want to slip between those thighs and take it out on her.

I disgust her? Nah, fuck that.

I reach for my glass and tilt it back. I need to get my mind somewhere else. The liquor won't do anything but numb it, but numbing is what I'm used to. It's what keeps me going. My cock starts to harden at the thought of a needed release. *Right on schedule.*

"What's up, dick."

I tilt my head up at the sound of Hemy's voice. He looks down at me and holds out a bottle of Whiskey. I can't help but to laugh a bit when I notice he's standing there wearing nothing but an American flag wrapped around his waist. He has claw marks all over his skin from the women grabbing at him. He loves it just as much as I do. He's a dirty mother fucker; like me. "What's up, man?"

"Not shit. You look like you need another one of these." He pours my glass back up to the top and leans against the arm of the couch. "You here to help me work the ladies tonight or what? It's a small crowd. A private party."

I look up at the small group of women that have started rounding up in the back room. Most of them look slutty and willing. I'm sure the thought of *me* fucking *them* doesn't disgust them. Most of them will probably be begging. How can I pass that shit up?

"Yeah." I take a gulp of my drink and watch as a few of the ladies wave over at us. "Why not. I have nothing better to do."

Hemy slaps my shoulder and stands up. "Finish that shit up and get your ass over there then. There's a certain someone that is asking for you." He starts backing away. "She has huge tits and a big fucking appetite. I'm pretty sure that's your type."

I can definitely deal with that. There's no shame in having a huge sexual appetite. I need a woman that can handle me. I like to fuck and I like to fuck dirty. The fact they get the ultimate pleasure in return is just the icing on the cake. If my cock is what does the trick, then why the fuck should I stop? It's not my fault I'm so good with it.

Taking a few more minutes to myself, I finish my drink and prep my brain by entering into fuck mode. It's what keeps my mind from going places it shouldn't while my cock is in charge. I stand and make my way over to the back room, ready to get out of my head.

Hemy has a group of women, groping his ass, legs and chest, while a few of the other women are waving money around and screaming. This is what we're used to; what we live for.

My eyes scan the room of women, until they fall on the one I'm looking for; the brunette from the other night. She's standing across the room in a tiny white dress that is hugging her every curve. She's by far the most attractive woman here and the perfect distraction.

Stepping up behind her, I brush her hair behind her shoulder and whisper, "I'm here. Now what the fuck are you going to do with me?"

She turns around in my arms and bites her bottom lip when she notices I'm shirtless; less clothes for her to take off. Her eyes look hungry. "I have a few things in mind." Her eyes rake down my chest and I can tell she's been wanting me for a while. Most women do.

"You want my cock?" I run her hands down my chest and abs until it lands on my erection; always ready when I need it to be. "I'll let you have it under one condition. There are no exceptions." I wait for her to look me in the eyes to be sure she understands me. "It's yours for one night and one night only. No bullshit after. Enjoy it and move on. I need to get off and I'm pretty damn sure you do too. Are we clear?"

She lets out a soft moan and nods as her hand gropes my thick cock, moving up and down over my slightly damp jeans. The look in her eyes is pleading for me to take her right here in front of everyone. She's about to tackle me right now and ride me right here in the open. Hell yeah, it's a huge turn on.

"Even better," she whispers. "I just want one taste. I've been waiting for this opportunity for a long time." She strokes my cock through my pants. "A *very* long time."

Seeing that Hemy has the room handled, I pick the leggy brunette up and walk forward until her back is against the back wall and we have a little privacy. She moans as I slide my hand up her dress and rub my thumb over her lacy thong, teasing her through the thin fabric. "Well, it's worth the fucking wait. Trust me." Wrapping her hair around my hand, I pull her head back, exposing her neck to my mouth and graze it with my teeth as I shove my finger into her entrance. It's so wet that I can feel it dripping down my hand. "You like that, huh?"

She moans next to my ear before biting my earlobe and tugging it with her teeth. "Oh yes. I love it, Slade. Don't stop."

I move my finger in and out, slowly at first before going faster and deeper. Her legs tighten around my waist as she moans out and starts breathing heavily. "This isn't shit. Just wait until I shove my thick, hard cock in there." I bring my lips up to meet her ear. "You're going to be screaming. You like to scream?"

"Mmhmm." Grabbing my face, she attempts to pull me in for a kiss, but I turn my head out of her reach. "Come on, baby. You're not even going to kiss me? I want to taste those lips." She leans in again and I lightly pull on her hair, stopping her an inch from my face.

"No kissing." I freeze as I hold her up against the wall angry with myself. I still have the taste of Aspen on my lips and I'm being a greedy fucking bastard. I don't want to share her taste with anyone.

What. The. Fuck.

"You know what. Never mind." I release her thighs and she slides down my body, landing hard on her feet. "I'll take care of myself. I'm pretty fucking good at it."

She gives me a stunned look before fixing her dress and combing the knots out of her hair. "Are you serious, you ass?"

"Yeah. I'm fucking serious." I push away from the wall and head for the door. When I look over at Hemy, he's standing there with his hard dick swinging everywhere. We don't usually get fully nude, but on occasion if no one else is paying much attention, we end up baring it all. He does it the most. He has the bad ass biker look down so when women see him stripping, they go crazy over it. Shit, one of the girls is practically sucking his dick right now. They seem to love the hard steel of his piercings almost as much as his dick itself.

Heading back over to the bar, I take a seat in front of Cale and grip the bar. I really need to get my shit together. "Three shots of Jack," I say stiffly. "Actually, make it four."

Cale reaches for the shot glasses and lines them up in front of me. "I'm guessing I'll be giving you a ride home."

"Yeah. Your guess is fucking right."

Yeah, and as soon as I get home, I'll be taking a shower to wash this day away.

"So what is Aspen doing then? She didn't want to come hang out here?" He looks up from pouring the shots. "She doesn't get pissed off easily. It must be a *Slade* thing."

Not really caring to hear what he has to say, I grab the first shot and slam it back before wiping my mouth off with my arm. "How do you know this chick anyways? She's not even from around here."

Now it looks like he's battling a demon of his own. I know that look well. I wear it with pride. "I was best friends with her sister, Riley, growing up. Riley Raines. They used to live here back when we were all kids."

Okay. I've heard him mention that name before. I can't remember for shit why, though. There must be something about these sisters that make a man go nuts.

Aspen fucking Raines. What a sexy name.

CHAPTER EIGHT
Aspen

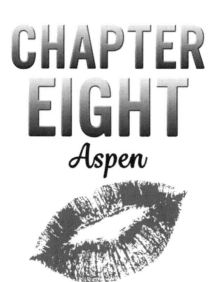

STUPID, PIECE OF CRAP, NO good vibrator . . .

I toss what I thought was my handy dandy vibrator down beside me and roll over on my stomach, shoving my face into the pillow. I'm so frustrated, I could scream. This cannot be happening. Gripping the plush pillow, I smother my face deeper and curse my damn vagina.

Is it broken? Seriously. I mean my vagina. Not the vibrator. The vibrator definitely had some kicking power left in it. I think that cocky, sexy, asshole broke it. Obviously, my vagina has decided it wants the best and has gone on strike until it gets it. I've never had this problem before him. Why now?

Rolling back over, I sit up and grab my panties, pulling them on with a sigh. A very frustrated sigh. After the orgasm I had yesterday, I'm ruined. No other orgasm I'll ever have will compare to it and it makes me so angry. It seems I've lost the control over my vagina. I've spent the last hour just trying to have a small orgasm; any orgasm and nothing. Trust me, I've tried both ways and what were the results? Nada . . . it's completely numb now.

It's definitely time to throw in the towel. It's not happening. Maybe I just need to make some breakfast, relax and try again later. I think I just have too much on my mind.

Yeah. That's it. I'm just mentally frustrated.

I stand from the messy confinements of the bed and grab my t-shirt from the wad of clothes on the floor, pulling it on. Exiting the room, I walk past Cale snoring on the couch and dodge my way into the kitchen. The boys didn't get in until at least two a.m. There's no way they will be waking up anytime soon. I'm surprised that I'm even up to be honest. I didn't sleep for crap. It was an endless night and a part of me wants to just crawl back in bed and force myself to sleep.

One minute I was checking my phone and the next minute I was checking the driveway. Not sure why I cared so much about when they were getting back but it seemed to drive me nuts. I haven't even gotten to spend any time with Cale and I've been here for three days. So far Slade has been my only real entertainment.

Lucky me . . .

My stomach starts growling as I begin to search through the fridge for something to cook for breakfast. Digging through the contents, I end up with a roll of sausage, a pack of bacon and some bagels. My mouth is practically watering just anticipating the taste. At least there's *something* in this house to look forward to.

Half way through cooking, everything starts to go horribly wrong. If I thought I was flustered before, this just confirms it. The bacon is popping grease everywhere and the stupid sausage is stuck to the bottom of the pan. The whole kitchen is full of smoke. It would be really embarrassing if the smoke detector went off right now. It's pathetic. I just can't seem to concentrate . . . on anything.

"Ow, damn!" I jump back when I get popped with bacon grease *again*. That shit really hurts.

"What the hell are you doing?"

I turn around to the sound of Slade's deep, raspy voice. He's standing there shirtless in a pair of low hanging jeans, showing off the muscles right above his . . . penis. His body is slightly damp as if he's just taken a shower, but I know he hasn't. I would've heard the water . . . I think. What is it about a wet man that is so sexy?

His eyes are dark and intense; looking at me as if he wants to either strangle me or just fuck me really hard. I can't really tell. I get a rush of excitement from both. That's really messed up.

Clearing my throat, I turn back around and start scraping the sausage off the bottom of the pan as if it's not a big deal. I just pretend I didn't mess breakfast all up. The last thing I want to do is see him standing there half naked, looking disturbingly delicious while judging my cooking skills. He looks tastier than this damn food. That's not what I need right now. "What does it look like I'm doing?" I ask, not bothering to hide my irritation.

When he speaks again his voice is right behind me, sending chills up my spine. His body is now pressed against mine, but not in a sexual way; in a way that makes my heart jump a little. Just a little. "Burning down the damn house. I hate to tell you this, but I left my fireman suit at work. I'm not prepared for this shit this early in the morning." He reaches for the spatula and hisses in my ear. "Now move out of the way."

Not budging, I reach for the spatula but he pulls it out of my reach. "I can handle it. Shouldn't you be sleeping or I don't know . . . kicking some skank out of your bed. I'm pretty sure you had a *late* night."

Giving me a stern look, he grabs me by the hips, picks me up and sets me on the counter. His lips are brushing my ear when he says, "I kicked her out last night. No girl sleeps in my bed. Ever." My heart sinks from his harsh words. He turns around and turns off the stove before throwing the spatula down. "If you needed my help then you should have asked. Is there anything you *can* do on your own?"

Narrowing my eyes at him, I get ready to jump down from the counter, but he steps right in front of me and stands between my legs blocking me. "What kind of a question is that? Is there something *else* you assume I can't do on my own?"

Running his hands up my thighs, he looks me dead in the eyes and smirks. "Yeah. Get off. I do believe you needed my help there as well."

"Fuck off, Slade. I don't need you to get off. Trust me." I place my hands on his chest and give him a little shove. Damn him; his body is pure muscle. "I can do it fine by myself. Now move."

He slides his hands up my shirt, lifts my body up and grips my ass in his hands. The skin on skin contact causes my breathing to slightly pick up. "Is that right?" Pulling me closer to him, he squeezes my ass and runs his lips up my neck. "Not from the frustrated sounds I heard coming from Cale's bedroom this morning. Those were definitely moans of frustration and not pleasure. Trust me. I know the difference." He slides his finger under the fabric of my panties and instantly I can feel the need for him to be inside me. He isn't even touching anything but the crevice between my leg and vagina.

What the hell?

Gaining my composure, I pull my neck away from him and shove him until he's out of my way. "You are so infuriating. Why are you such an ass?" I hop down from the counter and start walking away. "I'll clean this mess up later. I'm not in the mood to eat-"

"Get dressed and meet me outside in ten minutes," he says trampling over my words.

I stop when I get to the doorway and turn around to face him. "And why the hell would I do that?"

"So we can eat breakfast." He pushes the pan across the stove and picks up the spatula, tossing it in the sink. "Be ready by the time I'm dressed."

"Yeah. You're funny," I huff. "I'm good. I'm going back to bed."

"Suit yourself, but I can hear your stomach growling from over here. Stay if you want. I just want to satisfy your . . . hunger."

He walks past me and then jogs up the stairs. The muscles in his back flex and the deep scratches in his skin stand out, making me hate my damn body again for the reaction it gets from him.

Son of a bitch . . .

AGAINST MY BETTER JUDGMENT, I'M sitting across a booth from Slade with a piece of bacon hanging from my mouth. We both just sit here in silence eating breakfast and I'm thankful for that. I really don't feel like chatting with him. Not that he seems like the chatty type person. Actually, he's pretty far from it.

"Are you going to sit there and play with that bacon all day?" He takes a bite of his hash browns and then leans against the back of his booth. "It has to taste better than that crap you were catching on fire when I walked in."

Rolling my eyes, I point my bacon at him and start waving it as I speak. "I wasn't catching it on fire, dammit. Why are you-"

The bacon slips out of my hand and hits him on the cheek, causing me to stop and cover my mouth to keep from laughing.

Watching me stifle my laughter, he grabs for the piece of bacon, smiles and takes a bite out of it. "You think that's funny, huh?"

I nod my head and laugh. "Yeah. You should have seen the way your eye twitched when it hit you. It was pretty damn hilarious."

"I bet," he replies before shoving the remainder of it in his mouth. "Now eat. I have things I have to do today."

"Yeah. Like what?"

He takes a drink of his coffee and then holds the mug under his lips. "Lots of things. Some of them include: work out, run, grocery shopping, clean the house and then go to work tonight. The things that adults do. In between, I plan to just ride and get away. Get out of my fucking head and breathe a little. *That's* what I have to do."

I look at him a little stunned. For some crazy reason I just didn't take him as the responsible type. I expected that Cale took care of the things around the house. I have to admit, it's pretty sexy. I almost like this side of him.

"I'm done anyways." I reach for my purse and get ready to pull out my wallet, but he reaches over and snatches my purse away. "Umm . . . my purse."

Shaking his head, he sets my purse down and pulls out his wallet. "Never expect to pay when I ask you to eat with me. I asked you because I wanted to treat you to breakfast." He pulls out two twenties and sets them on the table. "Let's go then."

He stands up right as the waitress walks over. She's a young woman, maybe in her early thirties. She looks a bit stressed out as she keeps looking back at the counter. "You guys are all set?" She picks up the money and her eyes go wide when she looks at the tab. "Sir, it's only fourteen dollars. Let me get your change."

Looking over at the counter, he watches the two kids that our waitress has been sitting with in between her running around like crazy. "No, ma'am. Keep the change." He pulls out another twenty, drops it down and grabs my hand. "Have a nice day."

I don't even get to see the woman's reaction because he pulls me out of the diner too quickly and then jumps into his truck without another word.

I keep wanting to say something, to maybe get a reaction out of him, but I can't think of what to say. I'm still stunned speechless by his generosity back at the diner. He did seem distracted while we were there. I noticed he kept looking away from the table as if something was catching his attention. Now, I know why.

"Slade," I say softly. "That was a really nice thing you did for that lady back at the diner."

He looks away from the road with a distraught look on his face. He looks like he's beating himself up over something. "Yeah, well she needed it more than me. Those kids shouldn't have to be at the diner while she works her ass off for three dollar tips. It's not right. They don't deserve that."

I sit here and watch him as he drives. He seems a little worked up and I can't help but want to comfort him. I don't even know why. The urge just comes out of nowhere. His side profile is strikingly beautiful and the act of kindness that I just witnessed makes him even more beautiful.

Without thinking, I reach out and grip his knee, running my hand up and down his leg for comfort. He stiffens at first and glances down at my hand with a surprised look, but doesn't say a word. He just drives in silence, keeping his eyes on the road. For some reason, I keep my hand there the whole way home.

I rub and massage his leg while looking down at my small hand on his muscular thigh. It feels good under my touch; natural. It isn't until we get back to the house that I feel his muscles fully relax.

When he stops the truck and pulls the key out the ignition, he looks over at me and then down at my hand. He's silent for a moment, his body still.

"I need to get ready to go running. I think Cale has the day planned for just the two of you." He lifts my hand off his knee and sets it on my own lap. "I'll see you later."

I nod my head as I watch him jump out of his truck and walk over to the door. Why is a part of me feeling down for him? Maybe it's because I feel there's something more to him than I thought. That maybe he is a real human being after all.

Hopefully Cale keeps my mind busy today. I think I need the distraction.

CHAPTER NINE

Aspen

IT'S BEEN TWO DAYS SINCE I let Slade go down on me in the rain and I've been working as hard as I can to avoid him. Well, besides yesterday morning and the brief moment we shared in the kitchen earlier today. He set a full plate of breakfast down in front of me before popping a piece of bacon in his mouth, smiling and walking away. No words were exchanged. The only other interaction between us has been heated stares from across the room. When I say heated, I mean hot enough to scorch me; to heat me straight to my core.

The thought alone is almost enough for me to get off. He's so intense, I'm not sure I can handle being in the same room with him for longer than five minutes without getting wet; panties soaked kind of wetness. I'm not used to that kind of want and need. It scares me. Not to mention, I'm still a little shaken up from our diner experience. I can't quite figure him out. It's eating at me.

"...Aspen. Hey! Are you even listening?"

"Huh?" I look up from the pile of makeup in front of me to see Kayla hovering above me. I give her a forced smile and reach for the mascara. I've never had a problem with paying attention before. "Yeah, sorry. I was just thinking."

She leans over my shoulder and grabs for my red lipstick. "See. Now that's your problem. You think too much. You better not be thinking about-"

"I'm not," I cut her off. I don't even want to think about it. I've been in Chicago for four days now and haven't spoken to Jay since the first night. The only thing I'm missing back home right now is cutting people's hair and interacting with my clients. Other than that, I don't even want to think about my life back home. "I'm not worried about him. It's something else," I mutter. "Someone just makes me so angry and I don't understand why I am letting it get to me so much."

She gives me a knowing look and yanks my hair to the side. "Tell me all about it. Did you sleep with someone? Was it Cale or that sexy hunk, Slade?" She drops down beside me and watches as I coat my lashes with mascara. "I want details before we get to the club. You've been spending a lot of time with Cale. Hell, you could melt butter off the both of them. If I was single I'd take both on at the same time."

I roll my eyes at her and push her out of my space. "Neither one. I haven't slept with anyone." I look up at her and my eye starts twitching. My stupid nerves are getting to me and giving me away. "What?" I say as her eyes widen as if she's just figured something out.

Shit.

"You may not have had sex, but you did something sexual." She shoots to her feet and yells, "You, dirty little slut. You better start talking."

I stand up and adjust my short red dress. The material is so thin, it makes me feel naked. It barely covers my breasts and hangs just a few inches below my ass. I can't even wear a bra with this dress. Kayla picked the dress out this afternoon when we went shopping. It's the first real time we've had to spend together since I've been here. Her job and family life keep her too busy. I envy her. I want that in my life.

"Maybe I did," I mumble embarrassed. "That's all you're getting because I'm not having you embarrass me tonight." I look around Cale's room until I spot my black, leather strapped stilettos. I grab them, buckle my feet in and head for the door. "Ready?"

She takes a bite of her jerky stick and grabs for her purse. "More than ever. Alex is letting me cut lose tonight. Don't be surprised if you see my hands all over that biker looking stripper. Hot damn, he is fine. I swear he looks more like he belongs in a motorcycle club than a strip club. Lucky for us, he's in the strip club. Now, let's go."

I must not have paid much attention last time I was there because I don't remember seeing him. The only one that got my attention was Slade. My mind was too clouded that night and I was working hard to keep to myself. Well, not tonight, dammit. I'm out to have a little fun.

WHEN WE ARRIVE AT THE club, it is jam packed. We literally have to squeeze our way through the door and over to the bar. I've never seen such a group of crazy women before. I can't even see the guys because they're buried somewhere in the way back behind screaming women. I'm already starting to sweat just from rubbing against bodies.

As soon as we get close enough inside, I see Sarah is tending the bar along with two other women I have never seen. They all seem to be enjoying themselves, despite the crowd - they have waiting on them for drinks. I admire them. I'd be freaking out right about now.

Sarah notices me when we get closer and gives me a smirk as if she remembers me from that first night. I'm surprised that out of a crowd of people, she would remember me. I'm definitely not one to stand out in a crowd. "Hey, gorgeous ladies," she says with a wink. "What can I get you girls tonight?"

"Something strong," Kayla yells out over the music. She smiles and leans over the bar. "For the both of us. Especially her."

I nudge her in the side, causing her to yelp and move away from me. "Ignore her." I smile and grab for my purse, pulling out some cash. "Just give me a Vodka and cranberry. Easy on the Vodka."

Sarah smiles and reaches for two glasses, setting them down in front of her. I hadn't noticed before, but she's actually quite beautiful. Long amber hair and big blue eyes that make you feel comfortable and at ease. I'm sort of glad she's here. "So, you ladies are back for more of the boys of *Walk of Shame*, huh. Well, I don't blame you." She scoops the glasses full of ice and starts reaching for the bottles of liquor. "I'm guessing you're here for Slade." She looks up at me and runs her tongue over her teeth as if she knows without a doubt, that she's right. "Nice choice, honey."

The more she talks, the more curious I get about Slade. She talks about him and the others as if she's had them all. I'm not sure how to feel about that. I'm not even sure I should feel *anything* about it. "So, what do you know about these boys?" She slides our drinks in front of us and waves at someone behind us.

"I know they like to fuck." She throws her towel over her shoulder and leans across the bar so that she's closer to us. "And I know they're good at what they do. You won't find any better. Trust me." She winks at me and smiles.

Sipping my drink, I look beside me to see Kayla is hanging on every word out of Sarah's mouth. I've never seen her so curious. She's practically sitting on top of the bar ready to jump on top of Sarah. "So, you've been with all of them?"

"Kayla!" I can't believe she just asked that.

"What! I'm just curious." She grins and leans in closer. "So . . ."

Sarah just laughs as if the question doesn't bother her at all. She looks proud, as if her answer makes her feel good about herself. "I've been with two of them. Best experience of my life. Both at the same time and it was hot."

Okay, now I'm curious. *What! Two at the same time?*

"Details?" Kayla's mouth asks what I'm too afraid to.

Sarah raises her eyebrows and jumps up to sit on the bar in front of us. She's really enjoying this. To be honest, I'm a little nervous. "All right, you asked for it." She grins at Kayla and then over at me as I watch her with curiosity.

"Well, it was Hemy and Slade. We were at a party at Cale's house. I had been hitting on Slade all night but he was in one of his drinking binges so he wasn't really up for it. I finally gave up and was having sex with Hemy in one of the rooms down the hall. Slade walked in, drunk and looking for pussy. I've learned that look well. Hemy was laying on the bed with me riding his cock and without stopping, just looked at him.

At first I thought he was going to kick Slade out, but then he asked him if he was going to just stand there or join. I about died when Slade came stalking in and kneeled behind me on the bed, pulled his pants down, rolled a condom on and slipped inside my ass. I will never forget that feeling. Two cocks filling me at once. They never touched each other, but it was so hot. The only bad thing is, Slade has sort of a rule. He never sleeps with the same girl twice and my one chance wasn't even alone with him. Doesn't matter, he won't budge on his stupid rules."

Why does that bother me? I'm not sure I'm liking this, but I stay and listen anyway.

Sarah makes a face as if just remembering something else. "It wasn't until later that I found out Hemy swings both ways. Talk about sexy. You haven't seen anything worth seeing until you see two sexy as hell men kissing each other. I'm telling you, it's hot. Hemy just likes to fuck. Doesn't matter if it's male or female; although, I don't think he's much for taking if you know what I mean. Being with Hemy and Slade at the same time was by far my best sexual experience, but being with Hemy and this other guy came in close second."

By the time she's done, I'm sitting here with my mouth open. Should I be turned on by this? I'm not so sure, but I definitely am; almost jealous.

"So, what about Cale?" Kayla looks over at me while taking a sip of her drink. "I bet that boy likes to get it on too."

"Kayla, I don't need to hear about Cale. That's just weird. He's like a damn brother to me." I look up at Sarah, hoping she's done with her story. I'm not so sure I can hear any more of this, especially right before I'm going to be seeing the boys practically naked.

Sarah shrugs her shoulders and grabs for a couple glasses when she notices some girls returning back to the bar with empty ones. "He's a little tougher to take down if you know what I mean. All I know about Cale is that he doesn't sleep with women. He only pleasures them and lets them pleasure him. I don't know why. All I know is that all of these women are hoping to be the lucky one that gets him to go all the way. I don't know. I would definitely take him for a ride. I heard he works wonders with his tongue. I've never experienced it firsthand, but the women around here talk. When you're a bartender, you get all of the latest scoop. It's part of the reason why I love my job so much. That and those fine as fuck men. I can get off just by watching them. I can't say that about many men."

She pushes the drinks in front of the other women, then comes back to us. "All I know is that you don't come to *Walk of Shame* unless you're looking to fulfill your darkest, wildest fantasies. This place is dirty. The boys are dirty; addictive." She slaps her hand down on the bar top and laughs. "Well, have fun, ladies. Gotta get back to work."

I swallow hard and look away from Sarah while trying to process everything that just came out of her mouth. I guess when you're hot as hell and surrounded by a sexual lifestyle, it doesn't really matter who's watching or joining in. Slade . . . seems to like sex more than the average male and pleasures like a pro . . . like an addict. Still, the sexiest man I have ever laid eyes on. He's definitely trouble and I need to keep my mind off him.

"Oh. My. God." Kayla grabs my arm and starts pulling me through the crowd. "Did you hear her? Hemy must be the other stripper I was telling you about. That's insanely hot."

"I don't know, Kayla. This place seems pretty wild. You heard her. The boys are dirty. You better be careful before you find yourself in a position you don't want to be in."

She stops and turns to me. "What? Like you?"

"I don't want to talk about it." Pulling away from her, I push through the crowd, just wanting to get away and my heart instantly stops when I lay eyes on . . . *him.* Slade is standing shirtless with a pair of leather pants hanging low on his hips, holding a water bottle above his head.

His head is tilted back as the water drips down his flawless body and his hand works its way down where it cups his dick while he practically fucks the air. He thrusts and grinds his hips while a couple of women are on their knees in front of him.

His body is slick, sexy and hypnotizing; it's hard to breathe as I watch him move to the slow, seductive song. I can feel Kayla standing beside me and even her breathing has picked up.

"She wasn't kidding when she said these boys are dirty and addictive," Kayla breathes while grabbing my arm and pulling me against her. "Look beside Slade." I pull my eyes away from Slade to see a very attractive guy with long dark hair, brushed behind his ears. "That sexual predator there is Hemy; totally fuckable and I want to be his prey. I can't stop imagining him kissing another sexy guy now. Oh man, that would be so hot. I would pay good money to see that. I don't know why, but it has me turned on right now."

I focus my attention on Hemy in hopes it will distract me from Slade's smooth, very wet body. It helps a little. Hemy is very sexy in the mysterious, dark way. His dark hair falls just above his shoulder and he has a beard, but not an overly long unattractive one. It's just enough to scream that he's a bad boy with dark secrets, much like Slade. His body is perfectly sculpted and he too is covered in random tattoos. Even his neck has tattoos. He definitely screams bad and dirty.

Kayla and I watch as he moves his hips up and down, grinding in some thick woman's face. The woman keeps reaching out and scratching at his chest, causing Hemy to thrust her face away with his crotch. He's wearing nothing but a pair of low hanging leather pants, just like Slade. These boys are definitely killing it with those pants. They don't leave much up to the imagination since neither of them are wearing briefs underneath. I can tell from across the room. I don't even want to check on Cale. This is too dirty and sexy.

"You like looking at Hemy," a deep voice growls in my ear. "If he turns you on that much, I would let him watch as I fuck you. Maybe he could jerk off as you scream for me to let you come."

Swallowing hard, I pull away from Slade and turn around to face him. There's no humor in his eyes, just pure want and need. "Yeah. Maybe I do like watching Hemy." For some reason, I want to tease him; see what kind of reaction I can get out of him. "I can't stop imagining how hot it must be to see him kiss another sexy guy." I lick my lips and smile over at Kayla as she lifts her eyebrows, probably wondering where I'm going with this. "It's definitely got me turned on."

Slade tilts his head while wiping his hands down the front of his wet body. He's looking at me with a cocky grin that makes my legs go weak. "Does that make you wet?" He steps closer to me and without grabbing me, rubs his lip over my ear. "Does it make you think about . . . fucking?"

I nod my head and exhale. *Holy hell, he smells so damn good.* The sweat is only making it more tempting for me to run my tongue over his every muscle and taste him on my tongue. "Mmm . . . very much."

He stands up straight, sucks in his bottom lip and then turns to Hemy. "Dude, get your fucking ass over here."

Wait. What is he doing?

Hemy grabs his shirt and wipes it over his chest before running over to stand in front of us. He's even sexier up close. Full lips with a piercing off to the side, amber eyes and a sexy smile. "What's up?" He looks over at me and a dark look takes over his eyes. It's a sexy, mysterious look that says he wants to ravish me. Maybe he really is into sex more than Slade. That's hard to believe.

Slade notices me staring at Hemy and growls. "You better fucking enjoy this." He looks to Hemy and gives him a hard look. "Don't get any fucking ideas, man."

Hemy nods his head confused. Hell, I'm confused.

Next thing I know, Slade steps up to Hemy, grips his hair and presses his lips against his. I watch as their lips move in sync with each other's. Slade even makes sure to use his tongue a little just to give me a show.

Hot damn! This is so sexy. Instant wetness.

Slade pulls away from the kiss and grabs for my hand. Before I know what he's about to do with it, he presses it to Hemy's rock hard dick. It feels so thick in my hand and I somehow forget how to breathe. "See what my tongue does to people?" He presses my hand harder against Hemy's erection and starts moving it up and down his thin pants. That's when I notice he must have a couple piercings down there as well. It makes my heart beat faster at the thought. "This is what I do to people," he growls.

I pull my hand away while fighting to catch my breath. I am so turned on right now that I can barely stand it. I'm heated to the core and I feel that if my thighs rub together that I will have an orgasm right here in front of everyone.

That was sexier than I expected. Why did seeing Slade kiss another guy only make me want him more? Is it because I know he did it for me or because he wants to have me that bad? Crap, I was not expecting this.

Hemy looks at me and takes a step closer. I can't help but to look down at his erection. I can't believe that Slade put my hand on his dick. I'm so embarrassed and turned on at the same time.

Slade puts his arm across Hemy's chest and stops him from getting any closer. "You can go now," he growls.

Hemy gives me one last look, smirks and walks away.

I look Slade in the eyes as he places his hand behind my neck and yanks me to him. His other hand slithers down the front of my body and stops on the inside of my thigh. "I'm not even touching your pussy and I can feel the wetness on your thighs." He bites his bottom lip and leans into my ear. "Be ready for me to take care of this later."

Then he turns and walks away. He seriously just walked away.

"Kayla," I growl out as she smiles at me. "Don't say a word. I will strangle you right now."

Kayla throws her arms up and backs away from me as she watches Hemy from across the room. "You're so damn lucky," she breathes. "That was so damn hot."

Yeah, lucky me.

Both of the men have gone back to their screaming fans, giving us all a show. A dirty, erotic, breathtaking show.

Maybe coming here was a bad idea. Yeah. Definitely a bad idea.

CHAPTER TEN
Slade

THE FRUSTRATION IS SLOWLY BUILDING. It's been four days since I've had sex and after watching Aspen give me heated looks from across the room, I decide it's time to get her in on a little action; show her what I can do. I can't take her shit anymore. This is a fucking record for me and I need to release this shit and soon. She wants me and we both know it. I just need to prove that I know it.

I walk over to her and place my hands on her hips, running my hands up her curves as her friend watches me with a huge grin. Even her friend can see what my touch does to her. She's eyeing us up, giving Aspen the nod; the one that says she's about to sit back and watch; her own private show.

Backing her up, I nod my head to Hemy and he kicks the chair that's sitting behind Aspen closer to us. He already knows what I plan to do. I'll have to remember to thank him for looking out for me later.

I can hear the surrounding women screaming and getting excited as I guide Aspen down to the chair and place both her hands on my stomach. The women fucking love this chair and so will she. I'll fucking make sure of that.

She gives me a nervous look as I stand between her thighs and start grinding my hips to the beat of the music while slowly undoing the top of my pants. We wouldn't usually do this in such a big crowd, but I want her more than anything I've wanted in a long damn time. Even if that means fucking her right here, I will do it with no shame.

I pull my pants down my hips just enough so the head of my cock is exposed to her. Her eyes widen as I push her hands down further and lean down into her ear. "Like I said, it's against the rules." I suck in her earlobe as I guide her hand over my bare skin and squeeze her hand over my head. "But I want you to touch it."

Her breathing picks up as her hand starts caressing my cock through my thin pants. Each time her hand touches the head, I close my eyes and moan and so does she. It feels so fucking good that I could bend her over this chair right now, slide that dress up and fuck her; no regrets; just pure erotic sex. I don't mind giving a good show; displaying what I fucking do best.

"That's it. You like touching my cock with everyone watching? Does it turn you on to know you're the one sitting in this chair, groping my hard cock? All these women would kill to be doing this." I grab her hand and help her to smear my pre cum over the head of my dick. "See how bad I want you, Aspen?" I pull her hand away from my erection and bring it up to her lips. "I tasted you. Now it's your turn."

She leans her head back and closes her eyes as I brush her fingers over her lips, giving her a taste of what she does to me. It's so dark in here that I doubt anyone can see that the head of my dick is on display. She must feel the same way because she seems to be enjoying it as much as I am.

She moans and licks my taste from her lips as she rubs her hand up my erection, pulling me closer. She loves my taste. I can tell by the way she licks her lips once more, savoring the taste before opening her eyes as if she's just noticed the crazy crowd of women surrounding us. "Slade." She pulls her hands away from my body and runs them over the side of her dress, embarrassed. "I'm not doing this. Especially, right now. I told you to stay away from me, dammit," she says breathless. "I meant it."

Standing up, she pulls her dress down and pushes me out of the way. "Go fuck yourself," she growls.

She says one thing, but her eyes say another. I think I'll listen to her eyes. They don't lie as much as her sexy mouth. Biting my bottom lip, I bring my body against hers and pull one of her legs up to wrap around my waist. Then, I lean her back and slowly grind my hips against her aching pussy while tugging on her hair. I've been imagining this for fucking days. It would almost be too easy for me to just pull her panties aside right now and slip right inside her. The thought causes me to moan against her lips.

I can feel her leg tighten around me as her body starts trembling beneath my touch. I know and she knows that she's about to have an orgasm right here in front of everyone. It pleases me, knowing it's from my doing. I can get her anywhere and she knows it.

Thrusting my hips, I move slowly to be sure she can feel the head of my cock rubbing against her clit through her thin panties. I want her to imagine just how much better it would be if it were inside of her; deep inside of her and filling her to max.

I pull her neck up and grind my hips one last time right as her body starts shaking and her breathing comes out in short quick bursts. "I told you my cock feels good, baby. It's going to feel even better inside you, claiming you."

Pulling out of my grasp, she gives me a heated but angry look before slapping me right across the face. The contact stings, making my dick even harder for her. I've done her in and she fucking knows it. She can barely even stand right now and it has me so turned on, I may not even make it through the rest of the night without having to release this tension. "I hate you sometimes. You're such an asshole, Slade."

The women start screaming and throwing money as she walks away and dips into the bathroom. They all want their turn, but all I want is to finish what I started. She's mad, but it's not at me. It's at herself for wanting me. It's written all over her face; enough for everyone to see.

I'M STANDING THERE WIPING MY sweat off when Hemy leans in next to me and whistles while looking across the room. "Hot dayum. She is one fine piece of ass. I think we need to tag team that shit later. You can bend her over and fuck her while she sucks my cock. I saw how worked up you

91

got her while you were dancing for her. She needs a good fuck."

I bring my eyes up to see Aspen leaning over the bar, tugging on the back of her tight little dress. Damn, those legs are enough to hypnotize a man and almost make him forget where the fuck he's at and why he's there in the first place. Just one look at her and I can't deny that I want that all to myself.

"That, asshole, is all mine. I've already gotten a taste and I'm not sharing." I reach for the nearest shot glass and slam it back, closing my eyes as the slight burning sensation slides down my throat, giving me a temporary feeling of relief. It's nothing strong enough though. Not even enough to give me a buzz.

"Well, good luck with that shit, bro. It seems that asshole at the bar thinks otherwise." He pauses for a second as I open my eyes and look up. He points and grips my shoulder. "She doesn't seem too happy. You better take care of that shit before I do."

I growl as some drunken asshole grabs her by the hips and attempts to pull her into his lap. I can see, even from back here that she isn't into it. "Shit! I'll be right back. Start without me." I slam the shot glass down and take off towards the bar. I am so heated right now, I could break this mother fucker's jaw.

I can slightly make out what they're saying as I get closer and I am right. This asshole is definitely drunk. Not a good move on his part.

"I said no, asshole." Aspen reaches for his hand and tries prying it away from her waist while looking out in the crowd as if searching for someone. Neither one of them seem to take notice of me approaching. That's cool with me. I'm still going to fuck him up.

"Come on, baby." The guy ignores her and tightens his grip on her, pulling her down to his lap. This only pushes me further. "Look at that fine ass. I want it in my lap. We could go somewhere more private if you want."

Swinging her arm back, she elbows him in the face and stomps on his foot. "I said, let go!"

The guy stands up, pushes her and grabs his nose that is now dispersing blood. "You fucking bitch. I will-"

Anger boiling up inside me, I reach for the back of the guy's head and slam it down onto the bar beside him as hard as I can. The guy groans out in pain, obviously not expecting it as he reaches for his hair to try to release it from my tight grip.

Yeah, well suck on that, mother fucker.

"Fucking touch her again and I will break both your arms and make your small fucking dick unusable. Got it?" I lean in next to his ear and slam his head down onto the bar again to get my point across. Then I whisper, "Never touch what is mine again."

I look up with the guy's hair still wrapped in my hand and am not surprised to see all eyes on me as I stand there breathing heavily. It's not often fights happen in here since the majority of population is women. My bad, but he fucking asked for it.

Aspen is looking at me with a heated look as if by hurting this prick turned her on. *Well, fuck me.* It turned me on too. I didn't know she had it in her. I like seeing her hurt someone. It's hot; especially, while she's wearing that sexy little dress.

Licking my lips, I push the asshole's head down, release his hair and walk toward Aspen. Placing one hand on her hip, I look behind her right as her friend is approaching. "Aspen won't be needing a ride." I look up at Cale as he gives me a concerned look, just now realizing what happened. "Give me the fucking keys," I growl out.

Digging in his pocket, he looks to Aspen. She doesn't take notice because she's too busy still looking at me with a very confused look on her face. She doesn't know whether to slap me or jump on me and ride me. I'll take either one. "What the fuck, man. You're not even going to finish your shift?" He tosses me the keys, already knowing my answer, and I quickly reach out and catch them.

"Nope. I have better shit to do. Take care of this asshole. Get him out of here." Grabbing Aspen's hand, I drag her past the curious crowd and out of the bar. Once outside I swing my truck door open, pick her up and set her inside.

She still hasn't said a word and I know why. She knows she's finally lost the war within herself. I'm about to fuck her and even she can't deny the sexual tension between us. It needs to be dealt with and there is only one way; to fuck and to fuck hard.

The look that she's giving me is enough to push me over the edge. I'm trying to be respectful, but I may just say fuck it and take her here and now before we can even make it back to the house.

Fuck me.

CHAPTER ELEVEN

Slade

LEANING AGAINST THE SIDE OF the truck, I pull out a cigarette, light it and take a long drag. That mother fucker is lucky I don't go right back inside and shove my fist down his fucking throat. I never want to see that shit again. I can't. I just fucking can't.

I hear the sound of Aspen's heels hit the pavement beside me, but right now I'm too pissed to even look up. I'm standing there staring at my shoes, trying to keep my cool. If she opens her mouth right now, there's a huge chance I will bend her over and fuck her right now. I have way too much shit going on in my head; not to mention that asshole inside has just pushed me over the edge.

"Did you enjoy that?" Her voice comes out soft, but with a hint of anger. I'm not surprised. After what I did to her in front of everyone, I'm sure she wishes it were me she elbowed in the face. "You just can't resist messing with me and pushing my buttons, can you? I don't get it."

I take another drag, close my eyes and exhale. I need another moment before I even attempt to speak. Right now, I feel like a fucking animal released from its cage and about to pounce on its prey. The intensity of me wanting her is eating at me.

"You didn't have to save me from that idiot. Besides, it looked like you were pretty *busy* over there trying to juggle the slut squad. I have a feeling you're a damn pro at it by now."

Okay. One more drag and I'm good to go.

I take one more hit, toss the cigarette down beside me and pin her against the side of my truck. She looks up at me with a shocked expression, but doesn't say a word. Her eyes just keep jumping back and forth as I stare into them. "I did enjoy it." I lean into her ear and rub my bottom lip up her neck. "Just admit it, you did too. You think you can hide it, but I can smell it all over you." I slowly run my hand up the inside of her thigh, stopping below her panty line. "And feel it."

I am not a patient man and I've been waiting too many days for this. She better be ready. I'm about to pour all my frustration into her body because she's the reason I'm about to explode.

"You can't fucking hide it anymore and we both know it," I growl. "You want to kick my ass and fuck me at the same time. Well guess what," I whisper. "I'm fucking waiting."

I hear her breathing pick up before she places her hands to my chest and pushes as hard as she can. It only makes her angrier when her shove has no effect on me. She leans her head against my truck and exhales. "How do you know it's for you, huh?" I move my hand higher and cup her mound in my hand, causing her to close her eyes and moan out. "It could . . ." She moans again as I start rubbing her through the thin fabric. It's getting hard for her to find her words now. I like that. "Be for someone else. How do you know," she growls questioningly.

Sliding my finger under the fabric of her panties, I shove it into her very wet pussy and grab the back of her neck. "This is how I know," I assure her. "The way your breathing picks up and your body trembles under my touch." I shove my finger deeper, causing her to raise her hips and thrust against my hand. "Do you feel that, Aspen? Your body is ready to be fucked. It needs to be fucked by me. No. One. Else."

I grab both her hands and hold them above her head while pushing my thigh between her slightly parted legs. It feels so good between her thighs. So warm and . . . wet. "You want me to fuck you, baby?" I gently place my hand on her throat as I lean in and pull her bottom lip into my mouth and suck it, hard. She lets out a soft moan and nods her head as her lip slips from my grip. "Tell me you want me to fuck you. I want to fucking hear it."

Looking at me, she doesn't say a word, but the look in her eyes says it all. She lowers her hand down the front of my body, down my abs and grabs my erection in her hand. It feels so huge under her touch and I can tell by her little gasp that she feels the same way. I close my eyes and moan as she starts stroking it through the fabric as if she fucking owns it. Damn, that's such a turn on. It's all hers if she wants it.

Her hands start working on the button of my pants as she leans in and bites my nipple. She's breathing hard as she looks up at me. I'm so fucking turned on right now that I can barely contain myself. I feel like a fucking virgin about to get pussy for the first time.

What. The. Shit.

I press my body against hers and grab her legs one by one to wrap them around my waist. We both just stand there silent, looking into each other's eyes before I slam my lips against hers and claim them. I can't take it anymore. I need a fucking taste. I suck and tug, before slipping my tongue between her parted lips and sucking her tongue into my mouth. I never thought kissing could be such a turn on, but damn her lips feel so good against mine. I have to admit that I've wanted to kiss her since that day in the bathroom.

"You still haven't said it, Aspen," I groan against her lips while rubbing her hand over my hard cock. "You feel how big it is for you?" Her legs shake around me as her hand caresses my erection. "Just say the word and I will drive us back to my house and fuck you so damn thoroughly that this cock . . ." I force her to squeeze my dick as I thrust and bite her bottom lip. "Will be the only thing your body craves."

"Dammit," she hisses while pulling her hand away from my dick in a panic. "It's happening again. Put me down." She pushes at my chest and forces me to drop her to her feet. I have to catch her when she almost twists an ankle because of her high heels. "Just take me back to the house. In case you forgot." She jumps into the truck as fast as she can and slams the door closed behind her. "I'm pissed at you. Shit!"

"Nothing new there," I point out.

I smirk to myself while walking over to my side of the truck and jumping in. I'm no fool. She can play hard to get if she wants, but in the end she and I both know that as soon as we get back to the house and walk in that door, I will have her riding my cock as if her life depends on it. Her body is getting desperate and so is she. Right now she hates me and is fighting against wanting me. Well, she'll hate me even more after she sees what my body can fucking do to her.

We ride in silence, but I notice her press her legs together every few minutes while glaring over at me. She can't seem to sit still and she looks as if she's about to scream. Sexual frustration is one of those bittersweet things. It claws at you until you release it and there is only one way to do so; to fuck and fuck hard. I can tell she's trying hard to keep her eyes away, but they keep scanning over my body, imagining it being on top of hers. This seems to piss her off even more.

Reaching over, I force her legs apart and slide my hand up her thigh. I slowly inch it further up her smooth skin until I feel the wetness between her legs. Then I stop. I want to see what her reaction is. I want to see how badly she needs me to release her.

She gives me a dirty look, but spreads her legs wider for me as if waiting for me to go further. I could pretend to be surprised, but I'm not. In the end, the throbbing between their legs wins out over the voice of reason in their heads. When I don't make an attempt to move, she grabs my hand and pushes it away. "You're an ass. Do you know that?" She presses her legs closed and looks out the window. "Stop screwing with me just because you think you're God's gift to women. You're gorgeous and you have a rockin' body, so what. Stop using that against my weakness. You're the only person that can piss me off this way."

She turns to look me in the eyes and her frustration is so sexy, it hurts. Yanking her legs apart, I pull her closer to me and rub my thumb over her swollen clit. I really need to get her off because by the time we get back to the house, I won't have the patience. I'm going to want to fuck her as soon as we step through the door. Her pussy has been the only thing on my mind since I tasted it for myself.

She moans as I start rubbing small circles against her body, teasing her. I start out slowly at first before moving at a faster rhythm. She starts rocking against my hand, getting more desperate the faster I go.

"oohhh . . . keep going." She rocks faster. "It feels so good. Why do you have to be so good at this?" She moans out in pleasure while pulling at her hair.

"It's a fucking blessing. Trust me," I groan while trying to keep my eyes on the road. "You ready to come yet?"

She nods her head and grips onto the headrest behind her. "Yes. I'm ready. I'm so ready," she breathes.

"Ask me to make you come then."

She runs her tongue over her teeth in anger before digging her nails into my arm. "Will you make me come? I want you to make me come. It feels so good when you do it."

I slip one of my fingers inside while still rubbing her clit with my thumb. She moans and digs deeper into my arm, trying not to scream. "That feels good, doesn't it? You like my finger filling you, huh? Just wait until I ram my hard cock in there." I shove another finger inside her and start moving them in and out.

"Oh damn, you're so tight, baby and so wet. Damn, it's running down my fingers." I shove my fingers deeper, while moving my thumb faster. "So fucking tight. Oh shit. Scream for me, baby. Show me what I do to you."

I feel her body start to shake before she clamps down around my fingers. She lets go of my arm and grips the seat while screaming. She arches her back as I shove my fingers in one last time. "Stop! I can't take it," she breathes. "Don't move. Just . . . don't. Move."

It takes her a few seconds to catch her breath. I don't blame her. That was one intense orgasm. I'll be surprised if she'll be able to walk after that shit. I slowly pull my fingers out and suck them into my mouth, tasting her as she watches me with hooded eyes. She likes it when I taste her.

Fuck me.

As soon as the house comes into view, I pull off to the side of the road and slam the truck into park. "Fuck this!" Pulling the keys out of the ignition, I hop out of the truck, slam the door behind me and rush over to her side. I can't wait any longer. I need to be inside her before I fucking explode. I won't nut until I get a feel inside her.

I yank her door open and reach inside to pull her out. Before her feet can hit the ground, I have her wrapped around my waist and I'm heading for the door. I practically bust the door down while slamming my lips against hers, both of us breathing heavily while fighting for air.

I don't even bother shutting the door behind us as I walk us over to the stairs. I set her down on the staircase and spread her legs before ripping her thin panties from her body. My eyes slowly trail from her breasts, down to her pussy as I bite my bottom lip and moan. "It's so fucking beautiful."

I force my body between her legs and press my lips against hers again. She's kissing me with such anger and frustration that it only makes me want her more. "I want to slap you so bad right now," she breathes. "I hate the way you make me want you."

"Well, I fucking love it." I grab the top of her dress and rip it open, exposing her breasts to me. I knew she wasn't wearing a bra. I could see her hard nipples even in the dim lighting of the bar earlier. She gets ready to say something; to yell at me about her dress until I suck her left nipple into my mouth, causing her to moan out instead. "You want me inside you, don't you? Just fucking admit it."

Moaning, she grabs me by the hair and yanks my head back. "I hate you so much for making me want you. Me wanting you is the last thing I need."

"Well you don't hate me enough. 'Cause if you did, then you would fuck me; punish me. I want you to slap me, scratch me, bite me and pull my fucking hair. If you hate me, then punish me. I want to feel your fucking hate; drown myself in it. Then I want lick the hate right off your fucking body and taste it."

She yanks me up by my hair so that our faces are almost touching. Then she looks me in the eyes before slamming her lips against mine and digging her nails into my back. A burn remains in their wake, but I love the pain.

I can't fucking take it anymore. This shit is happening. I rip her dress the rest of the way off so she's lying fully naked beneath me. She looks embarrassed at first, but then relaxes as she watches me undo my pants, pull them off and reach for my cock. I stroke it for a second to see how much she likes it. Her eyes look heated as she watches me.

I stroke it a few more times before pulling a condom out of my pocket, ripping the wrapper open with my teeth and rolling it over my erection.

Not wanting to wait another second, I grip the back of her neck while sliding inside of her. We both moan as I slowly push it in all the way and stop to give her body time to adjust to my thickness.

"Fuck, you are so wet for me."

We're both panting now as I press my lips to hers and fuck her while backing her up the stairs. We get higher with each thrust until we're at the top of the stairs.

Pushing into her, I pick her up and she grabs onto the top of the door frame while I roll my hips in and out, fucking her as hard as I can.

Her grip tightens on the door frame as I grab her hair and yank back while pushing deep. "Fuck, you feel so damn good." I thrust into her hard and long, causing her to pull on the door frame, almost ripping it off. "You're so tight. Damn, my cock can hardly fit inside you."

The only sound around us is the sound of our heavy breathing and our sweaty bodies slapping together as I pleasure her. It feels so fucking good, but I want to get her in my bed.

"Let go of the door frame," I breathe in command. "Grab onto my hair, baby."

Squeezing her legs around me, she lets go of the door frame and grips onto my hair. Her hands rub the back of my head as if she enjoys touching me and wants more. It almost makes me want more. "Slade," she moans. "I'm going to hate myself after this."

Slamming her against the wall, I thrust into her while biting her neck. "Well, until then you can fucking enjoy it."

The louder she screams, the harder I fuck her. I've been waiting for this for too long and I'm going to make sure she never forgets the way my cock makes her scream. I want her to crave my fucking cock; to never think of another one besides mine and how it fucked her so good she couldn't think straight, let alone walk. I want my cock to own her fucking pussy.

We somehow make it to my bedroom door. I hold her against it, never stopping my assault on her body while turning the knob and pushing it open as I thrust in a steady rhythm. She grips me tighter when she realizes that there's nothing behind her to support her any longer. I love having her hang on me and touch me all over. Her hands are roaming my body, taking it all in and I love it. It only proves more that she has been wanting me as long as I have wanted her.

I take a few steps inside before tossing her on my bed. I quickly jump on behind her and flip her over so her ass is up in the air, facing me. I grab her by the hips, run my tongue up her pussy, then thrust into her slow and hard.

She grips the blanket and moans as I reach around and play with her clit. "You want to come again, baby?" I rub it faster, while pushing into her, filling her to the hilt.

She nods and pushes against me with her ass.

"Show me how badly you want me to fuck you then, Aspen. Fucking take your hate and frustration out on me. Show me and I'll make you come again."

I pull out of her and flip her over so she's looking up at me from her back. Her legs are spread wide as she takes a few deep breaths and then sits up. "You want to see my hate?" She grabs me by the hair and jumps at me so we both fall off the bed with her on top of me. "You're not the only one that has frustration to get out."

Straddling me, she slaps me across the face and then grabs my hair before sinking onto my cock and biting my ear.

Holy shit.

I'm so fucking turned on that I could bust my load right now, but I won't. This is going to last as long as I can make it. This feels too good to stop.

Grabbing her by the hips, I close my eyes and moan while she rides me. "Bite me again and I will pick you up, bind your hands behind your head and fuck you so hard that it hurts."

I don't know if she thinks I'm only messing around or if she really just wants it hard, but she bites into my ear again and tugs on my hair.

I flip her over so that I'm between her legs. Then I look her in the eyes and smirk. "You fucking asked for it."

She lets out a little yelp as I pick her up, hold her hands above her head and slam her into the wall. "Fuck me, Slade," she moans. "I want your *big* dick deep inside of me. I want to see how long you've been wanting me. I want to know that I'm not the only one that's been suffering."

Hearing her say those words releases some kind of beast inside of me. I've never wanted to fuck someone so hard in my life. She knows just the right things to trigger me and get what she wants. She wants me to make her scream again. I can't hold back. Pleasing her turns me on more than anything.

Shit!

Thrusting back into her, I place one hand around her throat while holding her hands above her head with the other. I push in so hard and deep that she screams and scratches at my hands. She wants her hands freed to punish me and I want the same.

I release her hands and they immediately find my back and scratch long and deep as my movements pick up. I feel her starting to tremble and I know she's getting close. Our lips meet each other's and I grab her face, forcing her to look me in the eyes as I make her come.

She moans and screams against my lips so I suck her bottom lip into my mouth and move fast and hard to finish myself off.

It only takes her kissing me hard and pulling my hair before I find myself busting my nut deep inside her still throbbing pussy. We both moan as I release myself as deep as I can. I'm not used to releasing myself inside anyone and the sensation is fucking fantastic. I usually pull out, but this felt too good to even think about it.

We stand here for several seconds, looking each other in the eyes before I pull out of her and set her back down on the floor.

I rub my hands over her face before leaning in and kissing her. She freezes at first, but then grabs the back of my head and slowly caresses her tongue with mine. It's soft, slow and hot. The most intimate kiss I've had in years. I'm not sure how to react.

I pull away from the kiss and back away from her. She watches me with a strange look in her eyes before turning away from me and placing her hands over her face.

She sighs before speaking. "I'm going back downstairs before Cale gets home. I'm sorry. This should never have happened."

I yank the condom off my dick and toss it onto one of my old shirts. I just stand there and watch as she walks toward the door. Before I can stop myself, I say, "Wait."

She stops and waits for me to walk over to her. Stopping in front of her, I cup her face and pull it up so I can look her in the eyes. I just have to look into them and see how I make her feel; see that I pleasured her beyond belief. "Your eyes are the most beautiful fucking thing I have ever seen."

She swallows hard as her eyes dance back and forth before she closes them, as if embarrassed. "In case you're wondering, no I didn't lose a contact. I was born this way, alright? I'll save you trouble from the silly question."

"I wasn't even going to ask you that. I noticed your eyes from the very first time I laid eyes on you. They've never changed. I'm not as stupid as some people. They're beautiful. Don't let anyone else make you think any different."

She laughs and it's the most beautiful sound I have heard from her. I've never heard her laugh before and it's nice to see this side of her. "Yeah, well I'm glad you're smarter than most. I would hate to have another reason to hate you. I already have too many to count." She pauses to push my shoulder and smile. "And thank you. Now I have one less reason to hate you. It's a start."

This makes me laugh. "Is that right?" I pick her up by her hips and set her on my desk. "I can show you a few good reasons not to hate me." I pause as I lick my lips. "Oh yeah. I already have."

She punches my chest, but this time it's playful and not out of pure hate or fuck me anger. I catch her fist and bite it to tease her. "You're such an ass. Do you know that?"

I nod my head and bite her harder while smiling up at her. She laughs and starts tickling me when I don't let go. "Ouch! Let go, Slade." She laughs and tickles me harder.

I didn't realize I was ticklish until now. I find myself squirming until I finally release her fist and let her jump down from the desk. She smiles at me and clears her throat. "Okay . . . I'm going now. Goodnight."

"Why not just sleep in my bed?" I grab her body from behind and pull it close to mine. I have no idea what I'm saying or doing. All I know is that it's late and I'm tired as shit. "Let Cale have his bed tonight. I'm pretty sure he's bringing some chick home. He's going to need the privacy."

She hesitates before spinning around in my arms. "You don't mind me sleeping in your bed?" Her eyes narrow as she watches for my reaction.

For some reason, at the moment, I don't. "Nah. Tomorrow you can go back to hating me from a distance. Tonight, you can hate me from my fucking bed. I promise it's a lot more comfortable than Cale's damn bed."

I watch her as she walks past me, smiles small and crawls into my bed. She doesn't say another word. She just looks up at me and keeps her eyes on me until I crawl in beside her and flip the lamp off. It only takes a few minutes before I crash out.

IT'S THE MIDDLE OF THE night and I try to roll over, but I can't. That's when I realize that there's a body draped over mine. My eyes shoot open and I sit up in a panic, causing Aspen to move but not wake up. I forgot she was in my bed.

I don't know what the fuck I was thinking when I asked her to sleep in my bed with me, but it's so unlike me. It must've been the adrenaline of finally getting her to have sex with me. That's my only excuse.

Stepping out of bed, I search for a cigarette in the darkened room, open the window and light it. I really need to get my shit together. My whole body is shaking and I'm covered in sweat.

I take a huge drag, close my eyes and let the harsh smoke fill my lungs before releasing it. I have to admit that she looks fucking beautiful lying there naked on my sheets and the thought of slipping back inside her is eating at me. It felt good. A lot better than I expected it to. I had never been so turned on in my life.

Fuck!

I put my cigarette out on the windowsill and take a deep breath while running my fingers through my hair, to keep from punching something. I need to get the fuck out of here. I need to go down to our gym and work this shit off. Like now.

Fucking get a grip, Slade.

CHAPTER TWELVE
Aspen

ROLLING OVER, I LAZILY OPEN my eyes and stretch; a
very long, hard stretch. It only takes me a few seconds for my
eyes to focus and remember where I'm at: Slade's room.
Panic sets in and I sit up straight, pulling the sheet over my
naked body. I was sleeping so well that I forgot where the
hell I was at. Not a good thing. Not good at all.

Shit! Shit! Shit!

I back up against the wall and look around to see I'm
alone in the big, quiet room. Slade must have gotten up in the
middle of the night and left. A part of me is glad. The last
thing I want to do is face his smug ass and listen to him rub
in the fact that he finally got what he wanted; not to mention
that is was great. It was the best I've ever had and I can't
deny it. My body already gave me away.

I tried so hard to resist. I really did, but he's too good.
He's damn good at getting what he wants and he knows it.
He knew I would eventually cave in and put my hate and

frustration into fucking him. It's what he wanted. He likes it rough and meaningless. Well, that's exactly what he got.

While mentally cursing to myself, I jump out of his bed and look around for something to put on. I really need to get out of his room before he comes back. I don't want to see him right now. I can't.

Shit. Why did I let him rip my dress?

Cale is probably downstairs sleeping on the couch and there's no way I'm going down there naked and risking him waking up to see me. I really doubt he needed the bedroom like Slade said. I think Slade just wanted another thing that he could be in control of. Well, I'm sick of him being in control. I'm out of here.

I rush over to the closet, almost tripping over the sheet, but I catch myself just in time and untangle it from my legs. Reaching for the handles, I slide the doors apart and step into his very big and neat closet. I'm surprised to see how organized he actually is; shocked actually.

I walk all the way to the back in hopes I can find an old shirt that he will never miss. I don't know how he would react to me wearing one of his good shirts. When I get to the back my eyes land on a huge row of business suits; very expensive looking business suits.

What. The. Hell.

I run my fingers across them while counting inside my head.

. . . 6, 7, 8, 9, 10, 11, 12, 13, 14. Fourteen suits! Why so many?

I look up to see there are more suits stacked up on the top shelf of his closet. I don't understand what kind of stripper slash damn bartender needs so many suits. Nice ones at that. These look and feel very expensive.

Pulling my eyes away, I take a step back and look around. There are stacks of shoe boxes with expensive brand names lined up under the hanging suits. Then, to my right there is a whole rack of ties. There is definitely more to Slade than I know; more than what he shows us. I'm definitely curious.

Gripping the sheet tighter, I walk back toward the front of the closet and look up at the shelf when I notice a pile of plain black shirts stacked on top of each other. I'm pretty positive he won't miss one of these.

I reach up and try to pull the bottom one out from the stack, but am not having much luck. I'm all the way on my tip toes and I can still barely get it in my reach.

Come on . . .

My fingers pinch the thin fabric and I tug, pulling the whole pile down with it, along with a shoe box. The shoe box lands on its side with the lid knocked off, causing a bunch of pictures and letters to fall out. I quickly struggle to gather the belongings and stuff them back inside before Slade comes back. The last thing I want him to think is that I'm snooping through his things. He definitely would not be happy about that.

After getting everything stuffed back inside, I am just about to replace the lid when a photograph catches my eye; one that has me very curious. I set the lid down beside me and reach into the box. My eyes scan the ultrasound, checking out dates, names and any other thing that may give me a clue as to why Slade has it stacked away in his things.

Helena Valentine, December 2011.

The baby is huge. It has to be at least eight months gestation. It's from over two years ago. It makes me wonder if this child is his. I really cannot imagine him with a child. It doesn't seem like him.

Setting the photo aside, I dig a little deeper into the box to find photos of a very beautiful pregnant woman. She has long, blond hair, sun kissed skin and a flawless smile. She looks happy; like the happiest woman on earth. She's holding her swollen belly, showing it off to the world as if she's the proudest woman in the world.

In a few of the photos, Slade is in the pictures with her, but he looks different; much different.

He's clean cut with short black hair, no tattoos and the most beautiful smile I have ever seen. I also notice that the scar on his cheek isn't present in the pictures. He looks so happy; nothing like the Slade I see today. He's laughing in almost every single one of them and even kissing her belly in one. He's wearing a suit in a few of them. He looks very professional and handsome.

I hate to feel like I'm prying, but it makes me wonder where this Helena is at. Where is this baby? Did he leave her and now regrets it? Is she still around, but a dark secret that he doesn't want anyone to know about? There are so many possibilities that my head is spinning. I feel lightheaded trying to piece it all together. Slade may be a lot of things, but I don't take him for reckless abandonment.

I'm sitting here just staring, in a daze, when all of a sudden I feel someone standing above me. My heart sinks to my stomach when I look up and see the hurt look in Slade's eyes. He's looking back and forth between me and the box. I instantly drop the photos and hold my breath, not knowing what to expect.

He's standing above me with his jaw steeled and his fists balled at his sides. His body is slick with sweat and his hair is dripping with water as if he's just worked out. His eyes are quick to change from hurt to pure anger and rage. I've never seen someone so angry.

"What the fuck are you doing in here?" He grips the door frame and squeezes as hard as he can. His muscles flex so hard that his arms are shaking and his veins are popping out. "Did I say you could go through my things?"

I scramble to my feet and grip the sheet against me. "No. I wasn't trying to snoop. I was looking for a shirt to-"

"Yeah. I can fucking see that. It must have been by fucking accident then. Am I right?" His jaw clenches even harder as he reaches for my arm and pulls me to him.

He looks me in the eyes for a second and I almost see them soften; a glimpse of hope that he wants to talk to me and let me in. I can't help what comes out next. "Where are they? Did you break her heart and leave her? What about your child?"

He takes a deep breath and backs us out of the closet before slamming the doors behind me and punching the wall. "Get the fuck out!" He reaches in his dresser, grabs a shirt and tosses it to me. I catch it while trying to keep my composure. "There. That's what the fuck you were looking for. Now. Get. Out."

I clutch the shirt against my body and watch as he leans over the dresser and takes a long, deep breath. He stays in the same position for a moment before knocking everything over to the floor and then pushing his dresser over as well.

He doesn't say another word to me. He just stands there looking the other direction, his body tight and his breathing heavy.

"I'm sorry," I stammer. "I-"

"I said get out," he says firmly. "Leave the sheet and go. I won't look at you. Just go." His voice rumbles as he grips his hair in his hands before reaching for his pack of cigarettes.

I can't stop watching him. My hands shake as I drop the sheet, quickly throw his shirt on and run out of the room, shutting the door behind me. I fall against the door and take a deep breath as I hear him breaking things and screaming from the other side. I didn't even know he was capable of feeling anything. I guess I was wrong. He's definitely feeling right now.

After a few seconds, I pull myself together enough to walk away. I don't know why, but a part of me wants to stay. A part of me wants in even though I know that will never happen. I want to see this part of him that I never even knew existed.

I quickly reach for my ripped dress and ball it up in my arms while running down the steps, past the couch and to Cale's door.

It's still dark and quiet so I doubt that he saw me. I quickly turn the knob and push the door open only to stop dead in my tracks when I set eyes on a naked Cale getting his dick sucked by some chick. He looks up while gripping her hair as if my presence doesn't even bother him.

"Holy shit!" I cover my eyes and fall against the wall. "I didn't know you were in here."

Cale lets out a soft chuckle. "Calm down, Aspen. You act as if you've never walked into this situation before." He moans before speaking again. "Your phone's been going off. It's on the dresser."

Keeping my hands over my face, I maneuver my way into the room and over to the dresser as quickly as I can. "I'll be right out. Shit!" I grab my phone and then quickly turn and rush for the door. Right as I'm about to walk out, Cale's voice stops me.

"You caved in," he says softly. "I hope you know what you're doing."

Without turning his way, I take a deep breath and exhale. There's no denying it. The proof was left on the steps. "I do. Trust me."

I step out of his room and shut the door behind me. My heart is going crazy right now and I'm in total shock and a little grossed out. I can't believe that girl didn't even stop sucking that whole time.

Seriously though!

I take a seat on the couch and take a look at my missed messages. My heart sinks when I see Jay's name across the screen. He called twice and sent a text message.

I touch the screen and go straight to the message.

> *This is a lot different than I expected it to be, Aspen. I actually miss you here. I'll see you in two days.*

Swallowing hard, I drop my phone down beside me and lay down across the couch. Any other day, I would be jumping to respond to his message. Well, not today. I just don't have it in me. The need is not there.

CHAPTER THIRTEEN

Slade

FUCK! THIS IS GOING TO be a shitty day . . .

I take a long drag of my cigarette and hold it in while leaning my body weight against the side of the building. I've been outside smoking for the last twenty minutes and I have a feeling it's going to take a lot more than just this shit before I'm able to collect myself enough to go back inside. My head is all fucked up.

I can feel my hands shake as I exhale and cross my arms over my chest to calm my breathing. My nerves are so shot today that I'm surprised I even made it out of bed to begin with. My mind hasn't stopped spinning since I kicked Aspen out of my room this morning.

What the fuck?

I toss my cigarette down, turn around to face the building and punch it repeatedly. What I wouldn't give right now for a fucking release; some kind of distraction. My mind is in such a haze I don't even notice the crackling of bones and splitting of skin. Does it hurt? Hell yeah, but physical pain I can deal with. I'm not good at dealing with *this* shit. The pain shooting through my hand does little to rest the demons inside my head. All it does is piss me off more.

I look up with guarded eyes when I hear some voices nearby. A few girls in passing; laughing and talking amongst themselves. The voices keep getting closer. I'm standing off towards the back of the building next to a dark alley that separates two buildings. It's not very often people come back this way. It's usually my safe place; a place where I can think.

"Is that you, gorgeous?"

A slim figure rounds the building and my eyes are quick to scan it out. Every single inch of it. A pair of long, slender legs lead up to firm thighs, followed by a curvy set of hips hugged by a barely there dress and a firm set of breasts. I know those breasts anywhere.

My eyes continue to marinate in the hot as hell female I recognize as the sexy redhead from the other day. She's no longer dressed in work attire. The perfect example of a little sugar and spice, that's for damn sure. She's in far less now.

Fuck me.

She smiles when she notices me checking her out. She's definitely enjoying giving me a good show and I'm enjoying the view. She found a damn good time to give it too. "Sarah told me I could find you back here. You busy?" She works her lips together, smearing her red lipstick while putting her cigarette out on the bottom of her heel. "I have some *extra* time tonight and was hoping I'd find you."

Wiping my bloodied fists on the back of my pants, I step closer to the temptation in front of me and look her up and

SLADE

down, taking her all in. "Are you sure you have enough time for me? This may take a while. A long fucking while."

Looking over her shoulder, she sends her friends off with a wave of her hand before turning back and flashing me a seductive smile. Her demeanor turns serious while checking out the bulge in my jeans. "I definitely have time for you."

She steps toward me, places her hands on my chest and backs me up against the building. I know exactly where she's going with this and I can't deny I need exactly that.

I pull out another cigarette and light it as she drops to her knees and starts unbuckling my belt followed by my jeans. She works fast at pulling them down my hips while rubbing my erection with her free hand. "Mmm . . . you're a big boy, aren't you?" She pulls my briefs down, letting my cock spring free from its restraints. Her eyes go wide as she licks her lips. "Definitely a big boy. I'm going to have fun with this one."

I close my eyes and take a drag as she moves in and closes her lips around my cock. She moves in a slow rhythm, swirling her tongue around while moving her hand up and down my shaft. She's a pro at this. The combination of the nicotine mixed with the suction is just what I need at the moment.

I moan as she starts moving faster. It feels fucking fantastic, but I'm not feeling the release that I should. This pisses me off.

Taking another hit, I inhale it long and deep while grabbing the back of her head and pushing it further down so my head hits the back of her throat. She grabs my ass and starts sucking faster; enjoying it.

I move my hips back and forth, fucking her mouth, matching her rhythm; looking for a release that isn't coming. Not even close.

Dammit! *I've had enough of this shit.*

Tugging her hair so she knows to stop, I pull out of her mouth, bend down and pick her up to her feet. I toss my cigarette down. "Bend over." I place my hand on her back and push her forward so her ass is in the air. Beautiful. She looks over her shoulder at me, waiting. "This isn't doing what I need it to do, sweetheart. I need to bury my cock deep in your pussy for the release I need. You better be ready to take it deep and hard." I bend over her and speak in her ear while pulling her dress up. "I have a lot of frustration to work out. Just a one-time release."

I turn her around so she can place both her hands on the building for support. She's going to need it. I slap the right exposed cheek, hard. She yelps and I press my front to her back. "You like that," I ask as I hook my thumbs under her panties and inch the tiny thong over her hips, letting them fall to her feet. Pushing back, I reach in my pocket for a condom.

My jaw clenches as I stare down at her slick pussy just waiting for me to ram my cock in it; to give her the same release I'm needing. For some reason, I don't feel the same rush as usual. As a matter of fact, I don't feel shit.

"Fuck!"

I toss the condom packet at the building and rub my hands over my face. I am beyond frustrated with myself at the moment. This is not fucking good. Sex has always been my way to cope. If I don't have that what kind of pussy am I? What the fuck am I supposed to do now?

She looks over her shoulder to see my face before she quickly stands up and pulls her dress down. She looks disappointed as fuck. "What the hell is wrong? Are we doing this or not?"

I shake my head while pulling my jeans back up and exhaling. "Not." I buckle my jeans and then turn to walk away while redoing my belt buckle. I need to get my ass busy with something. Fucking shots or something. Anything to numb this shit.

I storm my way back into the bar and over to Sarah. "Give me a fucking shot; the strongest you got . . . and quick." I sit my ass on a stool and watch as she reaches for a glass. She flashes a knowing smile while setting it down in front of me and eyeing me up and down. "What, Sarah?"

She shakes her head and pours me a shot of Whiskey. "Looks like you're not the only one here to drink your mind away." She nods behind me and leans over the bar. "Look behind you by Hemy."

I grab my shot and spin around in my stool while slamming it back. The sight in front of me makes my heart race.

What the hell?

"How long has she been here?" I push the shot glass in front of Sarah and stand up. "Another one. Fast."

Sarah sighs and pours me another one. "She got here right after you went outside. She's already had three shots of Vodka and a Vodka and cranberry." She watches as I slam back the second shot before speaking again. "She looks like she's having some fun with Hemy. My guess is . . ." She smirks at me and grabs my empty glass out of my hand.

VICTORIA ASHLEY

"That you already fucked her. Women always seem to go looking for the next guy to make her feel *wanted*."

"Yeah, well we both know she isn't getting it with that mother fucker. He's worse than I am. Shit."

I can already see Hemy working his bad boy charm on Aspen and even from across the room, it looks as if it might be working. The truth is, if Hemy wants to fuck someone he will fuck them one way or another. It's how it works with him.

He's over there with his jeans unbuttoned, slowly pouring water down the front of his chest while looking her directly in the eyes and fucking the damn air. From my angle I can see her hands reach out to touch his stomach. I'm not sure I'm liking this shit.

Making my way across the room, I step up behind Aspen and grab her arm to turn her around. It takes her a few seconds before she even registers that she's looking at me. The drinks are clearly setting in and I'm wondering just what the hell her reasoning is for being all over Hemy. "What the fuck are you doing here?"

Aspen laughs, clearly unfazed by my tone and yanks her arm out of my reach. "I'm getting a strip tease from Hemy. What does it look like?" She reaches for Hemy's jeans and pulls him closer to her. "Don't stop dancing on account of that asshole," she says with a scowl.

Hemy raises an eyebrow to me and smirks as he notices my eyes trail down toward her hands that are working their way down to his hard dick. She's clearly trying to push my buttons.

"Don't come over here and try to ruin my fun just because you're having a bad day. Clearly you have some shit

122

to deal with." She runs her hand over Hemy's cock while looking at me. Hemy seems to fucking like this. "Maybe Hemy isn't as big of a dick as you." She laughs and looks me in the eyes. "Well, he definitely has as big of a dick as you. Maybe he knows how to use it just as good."

Okay. Now I am getting extremely fucking pissed. I don't like seeing her rub his fucking cock one bit. It makes me want to kick the shit out of Hemy. Well, that's a fucking new feeling. "Too bad you won't be finding out. You're fucking going home. Now."

She yanks her arm away from me as I reach for it. "The hell I am. I'm having fun with Hemy. He's so damn *sexy*." She steps closer to Hemy and caresses his chest and abs. "And I bet those piercings feel . . . good. I've heard some hot, hot stories about him. Maybe I want to try him out. Have a little fun of my own for once."

Hemy goes to reach for her waist, but I place my hand to his chest and push him back. "Back the fuck up, man." My jaw steels as I look him in the eyes to let him know just how fucking serious I am. "Not a good time to fuck with me."

Hemy gives me a hard look before backing away and finding the closest chick to start grinding on. We may push each other's buttons, but we've figured out in the past just how far to push each other. We're not going that fucking route again.

"Are you serious?" Aspen reaches for her purse and starts heading for the door. "I really cannot stand you. First you fuck me and then you throw me out like trash and now you ruin my fun. What the hell goes on in your twisted mind?" She moves faster as I fall into step behind her. "Huh? Huh? What?"

"None of your business. All you need to know is that you're acting like a fucking fool. If you think Hemy will treat you any better than me, then you're fucking mistaking. He will take you home and call over a buddy while they both fuck you until you're sore. Then they will wake up and fuck you again. You will still end up alone in the end results. Hemy is not going to make things any better."

She yanks the door open and rushes outside before turning around to yell at me. "So, what the hell does it matter? It seems that no one wants me. I'm not enough for anyone. Might as well just fuck them all then. I'm so tired of it. So tired of everyone treating me like I'm worth nothing but sex. What is so wrong with me?"

I watch as she turns around and stomps over to her friend's car. She struggles with unlocking the door while trying to balance on her heels. "Don't you fucking get in that car." I stride over and yank the keys from her hand. "You're not driving."

She reaches for the keys, but I hold them up high so she can't reach them. She slaps my chest and pushes me. "Give. Me. The. Keys."

I shove them in my front pocket and push up against her until her body is pinned against the car. "No. You're not driving. You're fucking drunk." I pin her hands above her head as she struggles against me. "And you are fucking enough. We're all just fucking assholes. You need to know that."

She stops struggling against me and looks me in the eyes. I see a hint of her there but I can tell that she's pretty close to wasted. After a few seconds, she pulls one of her arms free and reaches into my pocket digging for the keys. I feel her hand brush over my cock and it instantly gets hard. "Give it to me, dammit."

I yank her hand out of my pocket and pin it back against the car while roughly pushing my body against hers. "I said you're not fucking driving. I'll call us a cab. Try reaching for those keys again and I will fucking tie your ass up with my belt."

"Why the fuck do you care? Now you want to be the good guy?" She laughs and pushes me away with her knee. I back off and give her the space she needs. She looks hurt now. I can't deal with that. "Get off me. I'll be over here." She starts walking away. "In the bushes waiting."

I don't understand why, but I just want to get this woman home and in bed; in my fucking bed.

BY THE TIME WE GET back to the house, the full effects of the shots must have kicked in. She's slurring her words and laughing at absolutely nothing at all. It almost makes me want to laugh, but I'm too fucking annoyed to enjoy this.

She laughs even harder as I pick her up and throw her over my shoulder. "My ass is showing." She starts tugging on her dress and squirming in my arms. "My thong! My thong!"

I slap her ass to stop her from moving. "No one cares. We're the only ones here and I have already seen your ass."

"Yeah. And a *whole* lot more." She begins pulling up the hem of my shirt, revealing my back. She inserts the tips of her fingers under the waistband of my jeans, lightly caressing my ass. It kind of tickles until she digs her nails into my skin and scratches upward. "I want to see more of you. Strip." She continues to scratch up my back, hard, causing me tip her back up.

I grab her ass cheeks in my hands and she instantly wraps her legs around my waist. She bites the skin on my neck playfully as she reaches for my belt. I start walking up the stairs toward my bedroom. "Take it off, dirty stripper boy," she says teasingly. "I love your body. It's so *sexy*. I just want to lick it and taste."

As turned on as I am by her biting me and trying to strip me, I keep my fucking cool and toss her on my bed before walking out of my room and slamming the door behind me. I can't let this shit happen for two reasons: number one, she's drunk. Number two, it's against my fucking rules.

Shit. I need a cold shower.

I take my time in the shower before quietly making my way up the stairs and to my room. When I walk in, I notice right away that she is sleeping. She's managed to strip out of her dress and heels and is now wearing one my favorite shirts. I have to admit, I like seeing her in it. She looks beautiful; like a fucking angel.

I reach for a cigarette and light it while pacing around my room and watching her sleep. She looks so fucking peaceful lying there. A part of me wants to crawl into bed next to her and hold her in my fucking arms, but the smarter part of me is reminding me of what a horrible idea that is. So instead, I dig out my favorite picture of Helena, grab the chair and pull it next to the window and sit.

I stare at the picture until my eyes blur. I haven't looked at this in almost a year. It hurts. It hurts so fucking badly that I can't breathe . . . but there is something making it a little easier. Someone that makes me want it to be easier. That thought scares me.

I must sit there for about an hour, in the dark with my hands wrapped in my hair before I hear her mumbling and moving around. When I look up, I see that her eyes are opened and she's staring right at me.

"Talk to me, dammit," she says.

I feel an ache in my chest at the thought of talking about it. I've been holding in my emotions for so long; for too long. Maybe it's time to get it out. She'll be gone in a couple days anyways. Maybe this will help ease some shit in my head.

Here goes fucking nothing . . .

I jump to my feet, toss the picture on the bed and try to hold back the tears. "Her name *was* Helena Valentine. She was my fiancé and was carrying my child."

CHAPTER FOURTEEN
Aspen

OH. MY. GOD.

I feel an ache in the pit of my stomach and a part of me feels like puking. *Was. He said was.* I blink a few times to focus my vision before reaching for the picture next to my feet and rubbing my thumb over it. It's moist and the color is smeared. It wasn't like that last time I saw it.

"I really don't want to talk about this, but it is starting to take every fucking thing in me to keep my shit together. I do everything I can to keep my mind busy. It's getting pretty fucking exhausting. I don't think I can take it anymore."

I look up at Slade and suck in a deep breath while taking in the pained look in his eyes. They're wet and I can tell it is taking everything in him to not cry. I can't even speak. I don't want to. I'm afraid to hear more. I'm scared to hear what he went through.

It's silent as he starts pacing. The silence is getting me so nervous that my stomach hurts. Not that the liquor helps any . . . but I feel totally sober now; wide awake and alert.

"I loved her with everything in me," he finally says. "I would have never left her or my child. Don't ever think that. It sends a flood of rage through my body. I may be a piece of shit now, but I wasn't always this way." He looks up toward the ceiling and rubs his hands over his face, clearly frustrated with himself. "We dated all throughout high school and I had known her since I was ten. She was my best fucking friend and I never had the courage to tell her how I felt. I went years holding it in, afraid that she would reject me and it would ruin our friendship."

He stops pacing, pulls out a cigarette and lights it before continuing. "She meant more to me than that. I couldn't lose her. I wouldn't allow it. Our freshman year I watched her date numerous assholes that always broke her heart. She always came to me for comfort and I was always there to take care of her. I promised her I always would be and I keep my fucking promises. One night after some asshole put his hands on her, I kicked the shit out of him and told her I couldn't take seeing her hurt anymore."

He takes a long drag of his cigarette and looks out the window as if trying to picture it all in his head. His voice is starting to break and I can tell this is tearing him up inside. I hate this.

"I told her I loved her; that I was *in* love with her. She was shocked as hell when I told her. I still remember that look on her face before she leaned in and kissed me harder than I had ever been kissed in my whole life. It was as if she were desperate; as desperate as I was. Come to find out, she had been in love with me the whole time and she was afraid of the same thing I was. From that day on she was mine. I took care of her." He turns to look at me. "And I never fucking hurt her. She was my life. I would have given my life for hers."

He places his hand over his face and looks down at the ground. I can't be sure, but I think I see tears falling. He puffs his cigarette and clenches his jaw. "If I could trade places with her I would, dammit. Fuck!"

He crouches down, resting his elbows on his knees with his face buried in his hands. "It should have been me. We were both in that fucking car. Not just her. Both of us, dammit!"

He starts shaking his head back and forth, hitting his head against the dresser behind him, as the tears come out steadily, dripping down his face and arms. "I didn't want to go anywhere that night. I tried so hard to get her to just stay where we were. It was New Year's Eve and all though I wasn't drinking, I knew others were. I told her. I fucking told her I didn't want to drive her home with all the crazy people that would be out that night, but she was eight months pregnant with our baby girl and she kept complaining she was uncomfortable and needed to go home to sleep. Finally, I caved in." He looks up toward the ceiling. "I'm so fucking sorry, Helena. I should have said no and put my foot down. You may have been pissed at me, but you and Hailey would be here right now. I would be taking care of you both; protecting you."

His body starts shaking as he looks back down at the ground and breaks down. He's crying so hard that I can't help the moisture building up in the corner of my eyes just from watching him. My heart aches for him. He's been holding all this pain in. That's not healthy for anyone. Not to mention the fact that he blames himself. No one should have to bear that pain.

I stand up and walk over to stand in front of him, but he doesn't look up from the ground. He just takes a quick drag and exhales. "The car killed her on impact; broke her neck. Dammit! All it did was throw me around a little." He brushes his fingers over the scar on his face. "I still remember holding her until the ambulance came. It felt like forever before they got there. I knew she wasn't breathing, but I . . . I just kept on yelling at her to hold on; that her and Hailey were going to be okay, but the blood . . . it was everywhere. Her seat was soaked in it, but I never let myself believe that Hailey wouldn't be born. I refused to give up hope."

He stops and chokes back a sob before whispering, "My life ended that night, along with theirs."

Without thinking, I drop down on my knees in front of him and place my hands on his arms, but he jerks away. I grab his arms again and pull them away from his face. He looks up at me through wet lashes while dropping his cigarette and putting it out with his knee. "You can't blame yourself for that night, Slade. Please, stop blaming yourself. You did everything you could to take care of them."

His nostrils flare and his jaw muscles flex as tears roll down his blotchy face. His eyes are distant and his whole body is shaking under my touch. His pain is too much to handle. All I want to do is help ease it.

I grab his face and rub my thumb over his scar as a tear slides down my cheek. He still hasn't said another word. He just looks numb now; dead inside. He's staring at me as if he's a bit surprised by my comforting him. "It's okay for you to talk about it. It's okay to let it out and ask for help to carry some of the burden. Let me help you." He starts shaking his head as he closes his eyes, tears still falling. "I know you miss them. That is nothing to be ashamed of. Nothing at all. Okay, dammit? The world should know how much you love them. Don't let the memory of your family die out because you're too afraid to talk about it; to remember. You shouldn't live life that way."

He clears his throat and looks blankly at the wall across from him. "Every day is a struggle for me to get by. Just the thought of losing them takes the breath right from my fucking lungs. It hurts so fucking bad. I never thought a day would go by that I wouldn't have Helena by my side. We spent every day together. Even as kids. It's not easy to just move on with life after losing the biggest part of you; like losing a vital organ. After that day, I just shut down. I gave up. Every day I feel like I'm fucking dying, over and over again. I can't fucking breathe, Aspen. I can't."

Feeling my heart break for him, I wrap my arms around him and pull him to me as tightly as I can. To my surprise he doesn't push me away. Instead he snuggles his face into my neck and wraps his arms around my head, letting the tears fall. So, I sit here and hold him for a while until the tears stop. It feels like forever, but I refuse to let him go. He needs someone. All of this pain has been consuming him and he's been living his life by numbing himself to the world; getting out of his own head.

Quite a bit of time passes, but finally, he pulls away from me and stands up. He doesn't even bother with wiping his face off. He just lets the last tear fall; unashamed. "You should get some rest, Aspen." He looks me in the eyes for a moment before picking me up and walking over to his bed. He stops in front of it and gently places me atop the mattress. "It's really late. Cale should be home soon. You can just crash in here."

He takes a seat at the edge of the bed and places his face back in his hands while yawning. I sit up and crawl over to him to place my hand on his shoulder. It's tense and he's still slightly shaking. "You should get some rest too. I am fine on the couch." I swallow hard while looking at his solid muscles though his snug shirt. They keep flexing as if he's struggling with something; as if he's fighting frustration. "I can stay if you need me to, though."

He turns around, wraps his arm around my waist and pulls me to him before laying back on the mattress. He gently brushes my hair away from my neck and snuggles up against me with his face against the side of my neck. His breathing is soft and warm against my flesh. It gives me goose bumps. "I need you to," he whispers.

My heart skips a beat from his words and I find myself wrapping my arms around him for comfort and to pull him closer; as close as I can get him. For some reason, being in his arms this way is making it hard for me to breathe. I have never seen this side of him and I'm afraid the feeling is too good for me not to want more. Right now, being in his arms makes me feel special. He's opened up to me in a way that I doubt he has with anyone else in a long time. This feeling makes me happy.

WHEN I WAKE UP, SLADE is gone. Just like he was the last time I stayed in his room. Except this time, I know he stayed the whole night because he never let me go. He held me so tight that I could barely move. Being in his strong arms made me feel safe and at home; something I haven't felt in a while. It confuses me.

I sit here for a while waiting for Slade to return, but he doesn't. It's been, I don't know, maybe twenty minutes or more since I've noticed him gone. A part of me worries that he's still suffering from the pain of last night and maybe he left to numb the pain. I've noticed the way he uses alcohol to numb the pain because, well, I did it last night. Pain gets the best of us all at some point.

I tiredly crawl out of bed and make my way down the stairs. When I pass the couch, I see that Cale is asleep on it. He must've assumed I was in his room when he got home late last night. Well, he was definitely wrong.

When I get to the bathroom door I stop, because it is slightly cracked open, but the lights are off. Last time this happened, Slade was behind that door and I'll never forget that look in his eyes when he saw me standing there. I'm not sure I can face that again. It made my knees weak.

Working against my nerves, I push the door open and take a step inside. Slade is standing there in a T-shirt and a pair of white boxers briefs. He's leaning against the sink while staring up at the ceiling. He looks lost in thought.

I hesitate before speaking. I'm not sure he wants to be bothered.

"I . . . I just wanted to check and make sure that you're okay." I step further inside and he turns to look at me. The look in his eyes is different this time. I can't tell exactly how, but just different. He doesn't speak; just clenches the sink and then lets go. "Do you need anything?"

He slowly walks toward me, his eyes focused on my face. His expression is calm and relaxed. I've never seen him like this. His hands reach out and he softly caresses my cheek before bringing his eyes down to my lips. "Yeah," he whispers. "You."

"What-"

My words are cut off when he tangles his fists in the back of my hair and gently presses his lips to mine. He kisses me soft, but with a want that makes my heart speed up. My lips part enough for him to slip his tongue inside and swirl it around mine. When this man kisses like this, he doesn't just kiss you, he owns you.

His muscles flex around me as he pulls me closer to him and slowly backs me up against the wall. I find my hands desperately seeking his body; just wanting to touch him in any way I can. Right now, we couldn't possibly get any closer, but I'm still trying; he's trying.

"I love the way your mouth tastes," he whispers against my lips. "I haven't wanted to kiss someone this much . . . in a very long time." He tugs on my bottom lip with his teeth before sucking it into his mouth and releasing it. "With you, I can't get enough of it."

Desperate for more of him, I slam my lips against his and dig my nails into his strong back. I feel him growl against my lips before he picks my legs up and walks to the right, stepping into the shower. He sets me back down on my feet while grabbing my hip and pulling me against him.

With his lips still pressed against mine, he reaches over and turns the shower on before guiding us both under the water. He continues an assault on my lips; kissing me so hard it's a little painful. The stubble from his lip scours my smooth skin, but at the moment I couldn't give a damn.

The water is cold at first, causing me to jump back, but he squeezes me tighter to him and causes a friction between our bodies. The radiation of body heat warms me up and it only makes me want him more.

His hands work slowly, pushing his T-shirt up my thighs as he works his beautiful lips against mine; teasing me in a way I have never been teased.

Every time his tongue caresses mine, I feel myself clenching my thighs to keep from going crazy. His touch and the taste of him is driving me mad; not only making my body want him, but crave him. Now I see why Hemy was so hard. This man is so erotic.

Both of us are drenched; our wet clothing plastered against our bodies as we stand here trying to catch our breath. He's now looking me in the eyes as he reaches for my thong with both hands and drops to his knees, gently guiding them down my legs as if I'm delicate and he's trying not to break me.

I place my hands on his shoulders and look down at him as I lift my feet out of them. After he tosses my panties aside, he looks up at me while running his hands up my thighs, followed by his soft lips. My whole body quivers from his touch and my breathing picks up as he gets closer to the ache between my thighs.

Just when I think he's about to pleasure me, he stops and stands up while wiping the water from his face. The bathroom is still slightly dark, but I can still see the steely blue of his eyes and the intensity in them is so great that I find myself grabbing the back of his head and slamming my lips back to his for more. They can't get enough; I can't get enough.

I feel his erection press against my belly as he cups my ass cheeks and squeezes. He picks me up and presses me against the wall. My legs wrap around his waist on instinct. His stiffness against my pussy sends a surge of pleasure and need throughout my body, causing me to moan out against his lips.

"Why does this feel so good," I ask breathless.

He runs his hands up my side and speaks against my lips. "Because it's with me," he breathes, "And I want you in a way I never thought I'd want anyone again. There is something about you that is different."

Pressing my body tighter against his, he rubs my pussy against his erection, making me want to scream out, even through the wet fabric. It feels so big and firm and it is still confined inside the cotton of his briefs. I've never wanted a man like this before. I want to touch him bare; undress him and pleasure him.

Loosening my legs, I slide down his front until I am standing on my two feet. I drop to my knees; my eyes level with his hard cock that is begging to be released from its cage. As I take hold of it in my hand, I picture what it felt like inside me and with that vision I lose control, having no other option than to release it from his briefs, so I do by hooking my small fingers underneath the elastic band. Pulling outward, his cock springs free, allowing me to pull them down his legs until they pile up at his feet.

His cock is standing at attention, commanding to be touched. It's the most beautiful cock I've ever seen. I run my hand up and down his shaft, brushing the tip of his penis once in a while to tease him. Each time I do this, he moans and bucks forward.

"Touching you drives me crazy," I whisper. "I want to feel you." He takes my hand and pulls me to my feet, pressing me against the wall. He touches my cheek with the tips of his finger, brushing my wet hair off my face. He lightly traces the seam of my body, stopping at my thigh and clenching it in his palm before pulling it upward to rest around his waist.

He brushes his finger of the opposite hand over my entrance, slightly dipping inside and running it up my folds before sticking it inside and slowly moving it in and out. He's good at pleasuring me and he damn well knows it. "Mmm . . . yeah. Touch me, Slade." I run my tongue up his wet chest, then up his neck, making my way to his ear. "I love you inside me," I whisper.

Pinning me against the wall with his sculpted body, he presses deeper inside, quickening his pace at an angle like a hook. Each time he slams inside, he hits a spot and it feels amazing. I can't help but to vocalize the way it makes me feel. "That's it. Don't stop. Please don't stop."

No man has ever made me come with his hand before, but I can feel it starting. I'm beginning to zone out as the feeling of bliss takes over my body. "You like my fingers inside you, baby? Do you want my fingers to make you come or do you want my cock?"

As the last syllable escapes his lips, he stops as I'm on the verge of orgasm. He looks me in the eyes with those magnificent blue eyes waiting on an answer. "I want your cock, Slade. I want you to fill me completely."

I feel his chest rumble before he grabs the bottom hem of the large T-shirt, pulling it off in one quick motion. "I need you naked for this," he says in a voice that makes me want to come right now. Placing his palms over my ass cheeks, he trails down both of my thighs with a quickness, picking me up and pressing me against the wall, aggressively. I love this side of him.

His eyes lock with mine as he lowers me to his erection and slowly eases it inside of me. I close my eyes and moan as I feel his thickness stretching me to accommodate his girth. He holds me there for a minute, being sure that I'm okay before he slowly starts moving me up and down his cock allowing the wetness to spread. He's taking me for another ride, despite the fact it's against his rules and I'm definitely not blind to this. It gives me a rush like nothing else and is hot as hell.

We both moan with each thrust; not able to get enough of this pleasure. It's beautiful, raw and erotic just like him.

Feeling him raw, inside of me, has my adrenaline pumping so hard that I forget how to breathe. I'm not sure if I want to. I just want to feel this moment for what it is and never forget it.

I slowly peel his shirt off him while his eyes take me in; every inch of me as if he can't get enough. His arms flex each time he enters me and his breathing picks up as he pushes himself deeper inside me. I lean my head against the wall, moaning, with each thrust.

My body becomes heated as the steam fills the shower, causing my head to become a clouded haze. Nothing else can be processed but the moment at hand. Between the water splashing against our bodies and the slow rhythm, I'm becoming hypnotized by him. It's a cruel pleasure. He's teasing me; ruining me. I can't concentrate on anything; only the sensation that is building in my body each time he pushes inside me.

He presses his lips to my neck while picking up speed and pushing harder and deeper as if he can't get enough of me. "You feel so fucking good, Aspen. This feels good." He places a hand behind my head and pulls it to him so it presses against his forehead; our lips barely brushing. "I'm about to go soon. I can't hold it in any longer. I need you to come, baby."

He presses his body weight against mine and starts thrusting into me hard and deep while swirling his thumb over my clit.

I feel myself shaking in his arms and moaning as I get close to climax. It feels so good that I have to scream. I do too. The pleasure is too much for me to bear internally. I fucking scream and grab onto the shower head almost pulling it off. I feel my release as I clamp down around his thick dick and squeeze my legs around his waist.

His reaction is to speed up and go even faster. He's ready to go now and for some reason I want to experience this in its fullest.

"I'm on birth control," I say out of breath.

He pauses for a second, presses his lips against mine and then fucks me so hard that I bite down onto his tongue. I suck it and he moans just before he pushes as deep as he can go and I feel him release his load inside me.

He holds me up against the wall, our lips twining as we both fight for air. Neither one of us speak. We don't need to. We just bask in our release, enjoying this moment of peace.

After a few moments, he gently sets me down, steps out of his briefs and we shower together with him cleaning me. With him touching me all over it's so hard to not want him back inside of me.

I can see it all over him too as he takes in my body with a look; as if he's ready to back me against the wall and own me. This want is too great for me.

He leans over my shoulder and runs his lips up my neck, stopping just below my ear. "I want you to come for a ride with me after we shower. I have things I want to tell you."

I nod my head and close my eyes as he attends to me.

I'm not used to this kind of treatment. I mean from anyone. Is this the way he always was before his life fell apart? Is this the person he has been fighting so hard to hide?

If so . . . then I'm in deep trouble.

CHAPTER FIFTEEN
Slade

I FEEL AS IF A fucking weight has been lifted from my shoulders. I've been fighting for so long, using every bit of strength I had to keep this shit inside; to not feel the guilt and pain of losing Helena and our baby. It's been almost three years since the accident. It's time I realize the pain will always be there. It's either learn to live or don't live at all. A part of me for the last week has been wanting to live. So, I think I'll hold onto that and go with it.

I'm just throwing on my shirt, when the bedroom door opens and Cale steps inside. He looks a hot mess as if he didn't sleep for shit. Not a pretty sight.

"Dude. What the fuck was all that noise a bit ago? You had some chick fucking screaming like mad in the shower. It woke my ass up and probably woke Aspen up. It's too early for this shit."

I raise an eyebrow at him while slipping on my Chucks and fastening my belt. "It *was* Aspen. Don't worry, man. She's perfectly fucking fine. Trust me."

He takes a step back and scrunches his forehead up. "Whoa, man. What the fuck do you mean it was Aspen?" He takes quick steps in my direction and stops right in front of me. "That has to be a fucking joke. I know you fucked her the other night. It never happens twice with you. Are you fucking with me?"

I place my hand on his shoulder and squeeze. "Nah, man. I'm not fucking with you." I smile and slap him on the back, almost making him fall forward. "I'm taking her for a ride on my motorcycle and chilling for a bit before work." I walk toward the door and stop to look back at him. "It's a nice fucking day out. I don't want to be cooped up inside."

"What. The. Fuck." He gives me a shocked ass look and runs his hands over his face really fast as if trying to wake himself up. "I must need to go back to sleep. I think I'm hearing things now."

"Definitely not hearing things. Now get the fuck out of my room, mother fucker." I nod my head and laugh as he walks past me, keeping his eyes on me the whole time. He's looking at me as if he's waiting on something. I don't have time for this shit. "What the hell is wrong with you?"

"Nothing. I'm just trying to wrap my head around this shit. Not only did Aspen *let* you fuck her more than once, but you *wanted* to."

"All right, man. Well I don't have time to stand here while you try to wrap your big head around this shit. I have to be at the club in three hours." I walk past him and make my way down the stairs.

Right as I reach for my keys, Aspen steps out of Cale's room, wearing a pair of faded jeans, a white tank top and some old Chucks.

All right. My kind of girl.

I grab her by the waist, pull her to me and suck her bottom lip into my mouth. She seems a little surprised at first, but eventually wraps her hands in the back of my hair and moans as I rub my hands up her sides.

I release her lip and look her up and down, taking all her raw sexiness in. "Shit, you're so fucking sexy." I press my lips against hers while backing her up against the door and cupping her ass in my hands. Right now, I just can't keep my hands off of her. "Fuck, just one taste and I can't get enough. I want fucking more of you."

"Wow. I definitely was not expecting this shit. This is way fucked up and unnatural. For the both of you."

Aspen pulls her mouth away at the sound of Cale's voice and clears her throat. She nervously looks me in the eyes and maneuvers her way out of my hold. "Umm . . . I'll be back in a bit. Slade is just taking me on a ride."

Cale lifts an eyebrow and leans against the couch. "You mean another one? Isn't two enough?"

"Ha. Very funny, smartass." Aspen shoots him an icy glare before reaching for the door handle and pushing me out of the way so she can walk outside.

I turn back to Cale and nod my head at him. "All right, man. We're out. By the way, you can stop worrying about her. I know what the fuck I'm doing."

He crosses his arms over his chest and stares at the door with a sullen expression. "Maybe it's not her I'm worried about." He turns and walks away without another word.

All fucking right . . .

When I get outside, Aspen is leaning against my motorcycle while staring down at her phone as if waiting on something. She shoves her phone in her pocket and smiles when she notices me watching her.

"You ready? Where are we going?" She's looking at me as if she doesn't know how to act around me. I don't blame her. Right now, I'm probably confusing the shit out of her. She knows my fucking rules. She knows I broke those fucking rules . . . and for her. I wouldn't know how to react either.

I walk over to my bike, grab my helmet and slip it on her head. There is something about a girl on the back of a motorcycle in jeans and a tank that is extremely sexy . . . or maybe it's just her on the back of the motorcycle. Once the strap is fastened, I straddle my bike and grab her arm, pulling her on behind me. "Hold on tight."

She wraps her arms around my waist and snuggles up close behind me. The unexplainable feeling I have with her against me doesn't go unnoticed before I fire up the engine and take off.

We ride for about an hour until we finally pull up at the same spot I took her a few days ago. The memory of her soaking wet in more ways than one instantly floods the banks of my memory. The reminder of what happened here last time already has my dick fucking hard and ready for more. I'd always wanted to pleasure a woman out in the rain. I can't deny it was one of the hottest things I've ever done. Not to mention, I was a little surprised she let it happen. That only turned me on more.

Fuck me. Now during a summer rain, I'll never be the same.

I help Aspen off my bike. As I get off, I take notice of the bulge underneath my jeans and adjust the enlarged area of my crotch. My cock is so hard right now that my jeans are almost not loose enough to contain it. I see Aspen looking down at my dick and swallowing as I push it down. She wants me again and it gets me so fucking hot just knowing that I have her ready for more so soon.

"Get over here, babe."

She seems hesitant at first, but walks over to stand in front of me. Her eyes are studying mine and she looks curious. I want to know what the hell this woman is thinking. What the hell, curiosity wins out. "Ask."

"I want to know more about your life, Slade. Why do you have all those suits in your closest? Please don't tell me they're costumes for work because I know that's not true. I saw the pictures of you wearing them. You looked . . . different. Nothing like you do today."

My eyes study her face. She's really serious about this. She wants to know about me. It may sound a little fucked up, but she's the first woman to ask me anything personal about my life. All that the other women wanted was a good fuck and they knew they would get it from me. I grew used to it; got comfortable and became accustomed to it. It became my escape; my addiction. It may make me sound like shit, but when you basically fuck for a living you get used to it; crave it and then it gets hard to stop.

For some reason I want to tell her. I want her to know more about me. "All right. I'll tell you." I pick her up by the hips and set her down so she's straddling the back of my bike just like the last time we were here. I just hope she's ready for this because it's a long fucking story and one I don't usually tell.

"I used to be a lawyer." She gives me a shocked look by widening her eyes, but stays quiet. I know, it's quite a fucking shocker from looking at the man you see today. "I worked for my father's Law Firm. It wasn't what I wanted to do. It was what I was expected to do. I didn't have a passion for it; although, I was one of the best. Everyone wanted me to handle their cases because they knew they wouldn't get any better. I was a damn good lawyer. I just didn't like it. I worked very hard; too hard. It got boring as shit and fast."

I grab her legs and yank her to me so her legs are wrapped around my waist and my hands are locked behind her back. "After the accident, I shut myself off from the world. I didn't leave my house for about a month straight. When that month was up, I couldn't force myself to go back to that life. No matter how hard my father pushed me, I just pushed back. I couldn't fucking do it anymore. I was tired of living life the way he wanted me to. There was only one option; to quit."

"A few months later, after draining the money I had in my savings account and not doing shit but eating, showering and sleeping, Cale asked me to come out to a party at *Walk Of Shame*. I hadn't been out of the house pretty much at all since the accident, so I agreed to go out and try to get my mind off things. Cale was dancing that night along with Hemy and somehow the women kept mistaking me for one of the dancers. They couldn't keep their hands off me. I hadn't felt anything in a long time and that night, I had such a rush that I was on some kind of high. It was the first feeling I had since the accident. I grew addicted to the rush and depended on it. It was my normalcy, so I took a job at the club and became roommates with Cale a few months later. I've just barely been getting by. First it was the dancing and the sex, then it became the tattoos and the pain I got from them. It kept me feeling something; made me feel more alive. When that didn't help me anymore, I moved on and it became the drinking. The alcohol was enough to numb it. It has gotten me by . . . until now. I want more though. I just don't know if I can have it; if I deserve it."

She scoots closer to me and reaches out to cup my face in her hands. I find myself reaching up to place my hands over hers as I look into her eyes. It feels nice. "Thanks for sharing that with me. I know how hard this must be for you. I also know that you don't open up very often. It means a lot to me." She leans in, hesitates, but then presses her lips against mine.

She gets ready to pull away, but I tangle my hands in the back of her hair and pull her as close to me as I can. The feeling I have right now is unexplainable. It's so fucking good that I could just kiss her all night and not give a damn about anything else. I haven't talked to anyone about my past and with her, she makes it feel so natural; so damn easy. It's like she's the medicine I've needed all along; the way to cope.

The feel of her in my arms and the taste of her in my mouth makes me feel . . . at ease. Just a little bit of peace finally; not enough to kill the pain, but enough to give me a little hope.

I pick her up off my bike and wrap her legs around my waist while kissing her long and hard. I want her to know that she's only making me want her more each and every day. At first, it was just a sexual attraction; the need to have something that I couldn't, but it's become more to me than just that. She's different than the other girls. She's more than just a fuck. She's addictive, but the right kind of addiction. I have a very addictive personality and she may be the thing I need to feed it.

A few minutes pass before she pulls away from the kiss and places her forehead against mine. We look into each other's eyes and I run my finger over her cheek.

"What," she asks. "Tell me what you're thinking."

"I'm thinking about how beautiful you are and the way you make me want more than what I have."

She sucks in a deep breath and turns her head away from me. Right before she turned away, I caught a look in her eyes that made my chest ache. There's something she's not telling me. I can tell.

"We should get going, Slade. You have to be at work soon. Okay?" She forces a smile and taps my chest so I know to set her back down to her feet.

When her feet hit the ground, she goes straight for my motorcycle and slips my helmet on. She's ready to get away from me. I don't like that feeling. Not one fucking bit.

I stalk over to her, pull her into my arms and make her look me in the eyes. "Tell me something about yourself that I don't know. I don't know shit about your life back at home."

She swallows hard and tries turning her face away, but I don't let her. I need to be able to read her eyes when she talks. "I work at a hair salon. I've been there for four years. I love it. Doing hair makes me happy. I just turned twenty three a few months ago and I have a cat named Puma. He's black and white and a pain in the ass, but I love him. I hate seafood. I eat ranch sauce on everything and have a passion for reading. I'm not much for the party life and would rather curl up with someone that cares about me and watch a movie instead of going out." She pauses to look down at my lips before looking back up. "There's not much else to tell."

I release her face and we both just stand here in silence. Something feels a little off about the way she's acting. Maybe it's just me. I don't blame her for not wanting to get close to me; especially, not knowing my intentions. I don't even know them myself. This is all new to me.

"Okay." I turn and walk to my bike, unsatisfied. "Let's go."

SARAH HAS BEEN GIVING ME weird looks all fucking day. I'm not really sure what's on her mind, but it's starting to get on my damn nerves.

"Say it," I mutter.

She sets her towel down on the bar and begins wiping it off. "Say what?"

I look up from putting the glasses in the cooler and study her face. She definitely has something on her mind. She knows I don't like playing these games. I'm not a fucking mind reader. "You have something you want to say. Since when do you hold back?"

Shaking her head, she turns away and starts working faster at wiping down the bar. "Okay, then." She drops her towel, leans against the bar and smiles. "You broke your fucking rules." Pushing away from the counter, she walks over to me and kneels down next to me. "Someone finally broke you. I'm in total awe of this woman. She's a goddess. I'm definitely jealous, Slade."

Grunting, I slam down the glass in my hand and stand up before rubbing my hands over my face. "Fucking, Cale." I reach for her arm and pull her up to her feet. "I swear he gossips just like a fucking chick."

She quickly grabs for a beer and places it in front of one of her customers before rushing back over to me. "He called me this morning to see if I wanted to get off work early; said he needed some extra cash. He got on the subject of Aspen and it came out. He's just as shocked as I am. Believe me."

"Yeah. Well, you're not the only ones. Don't even ask me to explain it because I can't. I wouldn't even if I knew how so back off." I lean against the register and watch as a few girls look at me from across the bar, smiling to each other. They're both looking desperate; watching my every move as if their lives depend on it. I'm sure it won't be long before they approach me and try to pull me into the back. I've had it happen more than once while working. It used to get me all worked up. Right now, I'm not even feeling it.

"Do you need to take a break?" Sarah stands next to me and eyes the two girls before nudging me. "I can handle the bar. I don't need you."

"Nah." I push away from the register and start checking the bottles of liquor to see if any need to be replaced. I need anything to keep me busy. "Not this time."

"Wow. Two surprises in one day," she says teasingly while walking back over to clean the bar. "I don't know how to take all this in."

"Yeah, well I can be full of fucking surprises. Trust me."

"Oh yeah. Well, here's another one. Look who's here."

I turn behind me to see that Aspen and her friend have just walked in.

Fuck me. She is fucking beautiful.

Aspen's eyes stay focused on me the whole time that her and Kayla make their way up to the bar. They both stop in front of Sarah and order a couple drinks. I see her trying hard not to look at me. I can tell it's a tough struggle for her.

After the way we left things earlier, I'm not sure how the fuck to feel about her being here. I don't get the way she was acting. I opened up to her and it feels as if she's trying to keep me out.

Fuck that. I don't need that right now.

Seconds later, Cale comes walking in and I focus my attention on him. Just the asshole I need to speak with.

The girls have taken their drinks and are heading over to one of the empty couches. Now would be a good time to give Cale a piece of my fucking mind.

I wait for him to step behind the bar before I get straight to the fucking point. "You have a big fucking mouth."

He looks at me and then over to Sarah. "You can take off if you want. I've got it from here. I'm sure you don't want to deal with this side of Slade."

Sarah nods her head and grabs for her things. "Yeah, I'll be more than happy to get the hell out of here." She starts walking away, but then stops to look back at us. "I already closed out my tickets. You boys have fun now; just not too much without me." She winks and takes off in a hurry, waving back at Aspen and Kayla.

"My bad, man. I didn't think you'd get pissed about it. You've never been secretive about your sex life before. It just sort of came out. It's a big deal. I still can't believe it."

"Yeah well, it's a big deal for me too so let's just drop it."

"All right." He looks over at Aspen and Kayla. "You do realize she'll be leaving soon, right?"

"Yeah. So?"

"She probably won't be coming back for a long ass time. There must be something special about her for you to let her get to you the way she has for this past week. Are you sure you're willing to let her go?"

I take in a deep breath and release it. I look up to see Aspen laughing at something some moron is saying to her. I feel my stomach drop as I watch her having a good time with him. "Yeah. It's not my place to have her stay. There's nothing going on between us. She'll be gone tomorrow and things will go back to normal."

"Really," Cale asks. "Is that why you're breathing heavy right now and your fists are clenched at your sides?" He studies me from the side. He's good as fuck at reading me. "You want to rip that guy's head off right now; especially, now that he keeps getting closer to her as if he's going to take her home. You're about to freak the fuck out. Admit it."

Fucking shit, he's right.

I jump over the bar, walk up beside her and nod at the douche in front of her. He looks a bit nervous all of a sudden. Yeah, well he should be. "What's up?" I step in between them, pull her to me by the back of her neck and press my lips against hers, immediately wrapping my hands in the back of her hair.

I kiss her hard; spreading her lips open with my tongue before picking her up and wrapping her legs around my waist. From the corner of my eye, I see the asshole has gotten the hint and has stepped away.

Smart move, mother fucker.

She moans softly before pulling her lips away from mine and running her tongue over them. She seems a bit shaken up by my bold move. "Umm . . . wow," she breathes. "I mean. What are you doing?"

"Kissing you. Isn't it pretty fucking obvious?" I pull her face close to mine before running my lips up her neck and stopping at her ear. "You like my lips kissing yours, sucking them and owning them. Just remember that."

I set her down and walk away. I'm heated.

Cale watches me as I make my way past the bar and outside. I need a fucking cigarette right now. The thought of that guy even trying to take her home has my blood boiling. I need to relax before I break something. I'm not used to this kind of jealousy.

Inhaling the cigarette in record time, I make my way back inside and try my best to focus on anything but . . . her. I never once thought a woman could be such a fucking distraction. All I can do is think about taking her in the back and fucking her; making her scream my fucking name. It's like my body can't get enough of her. I just have to touch her and taste her. She's in for it tonight. As soon as I get her ass home, she's mine.

It's been three hours since Aspen and Cale have gotten here and it's almost time for me to get the fuck out of here. I don't care what Cale says, she is leaving with me. She doesn't need to hang out here all night while he works. Her friend Kayla left about an hour ago; said she had to leave for work. So, Aspen has been going back and forth between hanging out at the bar with me and Cale and talking to some girls she met while getting a drink earlier.

By the way she keeps looking at me, I can tell she's just as ready to get out of here as I am.

"You taking off soon?" Cale's voice causes me to look up from wiping down the bar.

"Yeah." I toss the towel in the bucket and walk over to the register to see what tabs I need to close out still. "As soon as I close out these two tabs."

I look up just in time to see Aspen waving the girls off that she's been hanging out with. She laughs at something one of the girls says and then starts making her way over to us.

Just as she's about to walk up in front of me, some guy calls her name, stopping her in her tracks.

"Aspen." The guy has light brown hair, styled in the front and is wearing a black button down shirt with dark jeans. He's about two inches shorter than me and almost as thick in build, but is clean cut.

There is something about the look on her face that I don't like. She seems surprised and not happy at all.

She turns around slowly and rubs her hands down the side of her skirt. "Jay. What are you doing here?"

Jay as she called him, walks over to her and wraps his arms around her waist, pulling her body against his.

Without thinking, I take a step forward, about to kill this asshole for putting his hand all over her, but Cale stops me.

"Get the fuck off me, Cale." I push his hand away, but he just pushes my chest harder. "Back the fuck up. That asshole is all over her."

Cale takes a long, deep breath and then exhales. "Yeah well, that asshole is her boyfriend."

What the fuck . . .

CHAPTER SIXTEEN

Aspen

THIS CANNOT BE HAPPENING RIGHT now . . .

Jay leans in and presses his lips against mine while lifting me in the air. Without thinking, I press my hands to his chest and push away from the kiss. This is so unlike me, but he doesn't even take notice. "Damn, baby," he moans, while looking down at my breasts and setting me back down to my feet. "You're looking sexy today. It kind of makes me regret this last week."

Kind of? Asshole!

I hear something break from behind the bar before I hear Cale calling out Slade's name. When I look behind me, Slade is leaning over the register, gripping the counter, all of his veins popping out as his muscles flex. He looks like he's about to kill someone. I cringe at the thought of Slade being pissed off at me. I have no idea how I'm going to explain this all to him. It's not what it looks like; not exactly.

Jay looks over at the bar and shakes his head before slipping his hands up my skirt and cupping my ass. I instantly grab his hands and yank them away. I don't like the idea of him touching me sexually in public. When it comes from him it makes me feel dirty; always has.

"Jay. I thought you weren't coming until tomorrow. Why are you here today?" My heart races at the idea of leaving so quickly. I don't know why, but I don't feel ready; not one bit. "Why today?"

Jay flashes me his perfectly charming smile and grabs my chin, causing me to look into his brown eyes. They seem so dull compared to Slade's. "I'm here to hang out with a few of my boys. They're going out for a few drinks here soon. Figured I would come a day early and have a little fun of my own here in Chicago. Now that I see how incredibly sexy you look, I think I'll swing by later tonight, pick you up and bring you home."

"I . . . you should've at least told me. Called or sent a text. Something. What if I had plans?" I can't help my eyes from landing back on Slade. They can't seem to focus on anything but.

Jay laughs, bringing my attention back to him. It's not just a laugh, it's one of those laughs he does when he's making fun of me. I've grown to hate it. He can be such a prick at times. "What is the fun in that? You know I'm a surprise kind of guy and you have plans? I doubt it. Don't be stupid, Aspen. You know you never have plans that doesn't include me and that's the way it will stay." He leans in and gives me a quick kiss before backing away. "I gotta go. The guys will be meeting up soon. It's a good thing I remembered where you said Cale worked at. I love surprising you. I'll text you in a bit for the address. Be ready when I get there."

He backs away while laughing as if he still can't get over the idea that I may have plans. It makes me want to scream. I hate when he makes me feel this way. Once he gets to the door, he turns around and heads outside without another word. Good thing for him. I don't even know what to say or think right now.

I look down at the ground and take a few deep breaths, in an attempt to calm my racing nerves. I can't even look up right now. I know how bad this must look to Slade and I'm not sure he'll even give me the chance to explain. It's why I got so nervous earlier when he was spilling his guts out to me. I just don't know what to do. I shouldn't have pushed for him to open up to me. It's a bit hypocritical when I can't even return the favor. I shouldn't have let it get this far.

I stand here, not making an attempt to move until I see Slade's shoes come into view. I hold my breath waiting for what's to come next as I look up at him.

His expression is hard and cold; eyes so intense that it steals my breath away. "Outside. Now." His voice seethes anger and could cuts like a knife.

I watch as he walks away and yanks the door open before stepping outside. I feel as if I can't move. Why do I feel so fucking guilty? Slade is the one that pushed me to this point and he just wanted me for sex; nothing more. He used me. I play tug of war with the confusion in my mind, *but . . . then why*? Why do I feel like total shit right now?

I gather myself and start heading for the door. Cale tries stopping me, but I hold my arm out to show him that I'm doing this. I need a chance to explain myself. I can't stand the thought of leaving with Slade hating me. It's just too much and would eat at me forever.

When I step outside, I look around but don't see Slade anywhere. I catch a movement in my peripheral vision and he steps around from the back of the building with a cigarette in his mouth. He's pacing back and forth, not even bothering to look up at me. I can see him shaking as he pulls the cigarette from his mouth and blows the smoke through his lips quickly. He's really worked up over this and it somewhat surprises me.

He stares off into the distance for a few minutes, before finally walking toward his truck and nods for me to follow.

I take small steps while going over a speech, trying to think of the best way to explain Jay. It's not an easy thing for me to talk about. Once I get next to his truck, he backs me up against it and places his hands on either sides of me so his hands are pressed against his truck door.

He leans in close to my face; so close I can feel the warmth of his breath kissing my lips. "You have a fucking boyfriend?" His jaw steels as he looks me in the eyes. They hold nothing but pure rage. "This whole fucking time you've had a boyfriend and you couldn't have fucking said something." He slams his hands against the truck before punching it. "I opened up to you. I let you in and told you things I haven't talked about in years. I don't like cheaters. It's one thing that I hate. I know what I do isn't much better, but at least I'm always honest first. Fuck, Aspen!"

I take a deep breath and slowly exhale. I feel like bursting out in tears right now, but I won't let it happen. I won't. "It's not exactly what you think, Slade. You know nothing about what I've been through over the years with that man. You have no right to accuse me of being a shitty person without even listening to what I have to say."

"What? What do you have to say? That you just needed to get away for a bit and clear your fucking head and then I came along and you decided to just let me fuck you knowing that your boyfriend would never find out. Did you think you could just go back to living your happy fucking life with him? Is that it?"

I feel the anger building up inside as he looks at me accusingly. I didn't want this. I didn't ask for this. I will not be judged without him even having proper cause.

I push his chest to try to give us some distance, but he doesn't move. "Fuck you, Slade. Fuck you!" I push him again, but decide to give up. He isn't budging. "It was him that didn't want me. You want to know why I'm here. I'll tell you why. It's because *he* decided he needed to fuck other women for a while. *He* needed a little space before he could give me his full attention. He expected me to be the good little girlfriend while he was back home fucking who knows what. I was supposed to be here just clearing my head and trying to deal with what I had to do to keep him mine. Then, you fucking came along and I caved into you. I broke my own rules for you. I said I wasn't going to stoop to his level because I loved him too much, but you just had to come along and make me want you; Mr. Irresistible."

I give him another shove and this time he lets me push him away enough for me to escape him. I can't look him in the eye right now. I feel too low; the only thing that makes me this way. "We've been together for five years. I was afraid of losing him. I was prepared to do anything I could to prove to him that my love for him was strong enough to handle anything. It killed me to know that I wasn't enough for him; that he needed other women to satisfy him."

Clenching his jaw, he punches the truck and leans against it. "So you were just going to let him go around fucking everyone and then come back to you like nothing ever happened?"

"Yeah, well. If you must know, I knew how he was to begin with and I let myself fall for him anyways. He was the kind of guy always out to find the next best *fuck;* staying out late at night and not coming home sometimes. All the lies. The fucking lies." I stop to wipe a tear off as it falls down my cheek.

I hate letting people see me breakdown. I hate showing what Jay does to me. "All I wanted was for a chance to make that change. I thought if I did this . . . that . . . that he would finally just be mine; that he would love me with everything in him just as I have loved him all along. I thought that I could be enough for once."

It's silent for a few seconds before once again, I am pushed up against his truck with his body blocking me in. He wraps his hands in the back of my hair and pulls my face close to his so our lips are almost touching. "If he doesn't see that you're enough, then he isn't fucking worth it. He's fucking blind. You deserve better." He pauses and his eyes lock with mine. "Tell me you're not going back with him."

"Yes," I whisper. "I have to."

He presses his body against mine and his arms flex as his grip on my hair tightens. "No you don't. Fuck him. He doesn't deserve you. You deserve someone better than him . . . better than the both of us, but I'm fucking stingy."

162

He runs his hands through my hair and brushes his lips against mine. "Stay here, Aspen." His breath softly caresses my lips as his breathing picks up. "Don't leave with him. Let me give you a reason to stay."

I sigh against his lips, fighting myself. "It's not that easy. I can't just throw five years away. We have a lot of history. We live together. He was my first. I can't just walk away."

"How do you feel about me," he growls.

"It was fun, Slade," I manage to whisper.

Pushing me harder against his truck, he leans into my ear. "That wasn't the fucking question. Fuck!"

Feeling trapped, I slap him across the face. I don't know why. I'm just so fucking scared to answer this question; scared of knowing the answer. He always finds a way to push me.

"You like that? Did it fucking feel good?" He presses his erection against me, causing me to moan against his lips. "Harder, dammit."

Completely lost in the moment, I slap him as hard as I can across the face. It feels good to let my frustration out. Not to mention the fact that his dick flexes from my hit. This man turns me on like no other man can. I'm completely breathless; lost to him.

Without even giving me a second to register his reaction, he picks me up and wraps my legs around his waist. "Here is your reason to stay."

His hand works fast to pull out his erection before he slips my panties to the side and pushes himself deep inside me. He stops for a moment before rocking his hips back and forth and slamming his lips against mine. My legs tighten around him as my whole body shakes from the feel of him filling me; stretching me.

"Let me make you feel this way every day." He pushes in deeper before slowly pulling it out and lifting my hands above my head. I'm so turned on right now that I could care less if someone catches us. "Does he makes you feel this way? Does he fuck you as good as I do?"

I shake my head, but don't answer him. I can't. I can't speak.

"Say it. I want to hear you fucking say it." He leans in against my mouth while rolling his hips in and out, giving me pleasure so intense I feel as if I can't even breathe. I'm overwhelmed by this man; completely stunned. "Say it, babe."

"No," I moan out as he lifts me with his hips and starts moving a little faster. Our bodies are so close that there is no space between us. We're both desperate for this moment; our last. "No one has." I lean my head over his shoulder and dig my nails into his back as he works his hips on me.

"Then stay," he whispers. "Give me a chance to change."

I shake my head, but he presses his lips against mine, claiming my mouth with his. Once again, this man completely owns me. At this moment, I am almost willing to give him everything; not just my body, but my heart.

With one arm wrapped behind my head, he grips my hip with the other while fucking me hard; rolling his hips and slamming hard into me. He can't handle taking it slow at the moment and to be honest, neither can I.

"Slade," I moan out, as my body bounces with each thrust of his strong hips. "Fuck . . ." I grip his hair in my hands and scream out as I feel my orgasm building. The consistent thrusts of his hips and the way he pushes me against the truck with each deep shove, has me ready to explode. "I'm about to come . . . oh shit." I feel myself clamp around his dick and this only causes his movement to pick up.

I can feel the truck start to move from behind me as he puts all of his anger and frustration into fucking me. His grip on my neck tightens before he moans out and I feel his dick throb as he releases himself inside me. Breathing heavily, we both relax into each other with our eyes locked. I can't turn away from the beauty of this man in front of me; I don't want to.

Shit. Why does having him cum inside me turn me on and make me want him even more? I'm so confused.

It's silent with him still inside me as he leans in once more and presses his lips to mine. They're soft and sweet, making me want more of them. I always want more. He's like an addiction. Everything about him just calls out for me; my body needing him to survive. He's an addiction I'll have to break. I have no choice. Too bad, I know guys like him will never change. Jay didn't. I won't start over with another man that's just like Jay.

When he pulls away from the kiss, he looks me in the eyes and sighs. He can see my guilt written all over me. He could probably even taste it in our kiss. "You're still leaving, aren't you?"

I nod and turn my head away. I can't do this right now.

"Fucking shit."

He pulls out of me and gently sets me back down to my feet while pulling his jeans back up. "I don't blame you for not trusting me," he says stiffly. "I don't even trust myself. I don't know how the fuck I feel. All I know is that with you . . . I feel something and I don't want to give that up." He looks away before opening the door for me to get in. "I guess I'll have to. Me wanting to change isn't good enough and I fucking get that, but I can't make any promises. I won't make one that I know I can't keep."

I feel a burning sensation in my chest and it becomes hard to breathe. It's taking everything in me not to cry right now. As wrong as it was, we both needed that one last time. It's unfortunate that it felt even better than the last two. I will forever be fucked after leaving here. Slade isn't someone you can easily forget about. I already feel that; the pain is too strong to ignore.

I HAVEN'T SPOKEN TO SLADE since we got back to the house a couple of hours ago. I decided to lock myself up in Cale's room and hide. I can't face him at the moment, because seeing him will only make me want to change my mind about going. I can't stay though. He'll only hurt me more than Jay has. Jay made a promise to me this time. I have to believe for the sake of our relationship that he means it. I've held on for five years, it has to be worth something.

Right . . .

I'm sitting here on Cale's bed with my suitcase next to me, staring up at the ceiling, when my phone goes off. My hand shakes as I go to reach for it because I know my time is up. I'm not ready yet. A big part of me is holding me back and telling me to stay.

The look in Slade's eyes was almost enough to convince me he wanted me. I could see the struggle within himself while he was asking me to stay. Asking a girl to stay with him is not something he's used to. I think we both know that it wouldn't last. I couldn't commit myself to the pain of losing a man as great as him. I already feel attached and I barely know him. I can't even imagine how I could feel in a few months. I would fall hard and fast . . . right on my face.

I have to go. Home is where I need to be.

I already know that Jay is outside because I hear a car door slam. He's most likely opening the trunk for my luggage. I just hope Slade didn't hear it, because I can't face seeing the hurt in his eyes. He didn't speak to me the whole way back to the house. It killed me. I just need to slip out of here unnoticed. I can't let my heart break anymore tonight.

I grab my suitcase, stand up and drag it over to the door. When I open the door, I look around but don't see Slade anywhere. I should be happy.

Right?

I find myself standing here for a moment, not wanting to move. I feel stuck. I allow myself a few moments of pity, suck it up and make my way outside. The first thing I notice is that Slade's motorcycle is gone. Not sure how I missed him leaving, but he's gone and the ache in my chest returns. I'll probably never see him again. The thought kills me.

Why does it hurt so much? Why do I wish he was here so I could see him one last time?

Jay stands next to the trunk, but doesn't make a move to help me as I drag my suitcase across the ground. Usually, this wouldn't bother me because I'm used to him being this way, but right now, it bothers me. It bothers me a lot. Slade may be all tough and closed off, but he would help me without a second thought. I know that and I love that about him. He's more than what he shows the world. There's a really great side to him that I love and want more of.

Dammit, this is so hard.

I feel numb and closed off as I step up beside Jay and look at him. I thought I would be happy for this moment . . . but I'm not. I'm fucking miserable right now. Seeing him is doing nothing but making me angry. The feeling of wanting to kiss him has now been replaced with wanting to punch him. Unlike Slade, he wouldn't get off on it.

Fucking Slade. Why can't I stop thinking about him?

I stop and look around as if I expect Slade to just pull up on his bike, jump off and kiss me; save me from this possible mistake. The thought gives me the ultimate rush like it did when he kissed me in the bar with the assumption that guy was trying to pick me up. I loved that. It made me feel sexy and wanted. Something I've never really felt with Jay.

What the hell is wrong with me?

"Come on," he says while looking down at his phone impatiently. "I have to be to work early and it's a long drive."

I let out a soft breath and struggle with tossing my suitcase into the back. He doesn't even notice. He's too busy on his damn phone. I really feel a lot of hate for him right now; enough to almost stay.

I get ready to say something, but he looks up and smiles. It's the sweet smile that I fell in love with. "Missed you, gorgeous."

I feel a little bit of my anger fade, but not enough. "I missed you too," I say while shutting the trunk and walking over to get inside the car. I feel like shit because to be honest with myself, I don't mean it; not one bit of me.

I just hope I'm not making the biggest mistake of my life

CHAPTER
SEVENTEEN
Slade

Two weeks later . . .

IT'S BEEN TWO WEEKS SINCE Aspen left and I still feel like the biggest ass for not fighting harder for her to stay. The one thing that made my life worth a shit I let slip through my fingers. I couldn't even face her. Instead, I left. I couldn't stand to stick around while she packed her shit to leave. I fucking left and rode for hours just thinking back on my life and all the fucked up things I have done over the past couple of years. It took her for me to realize that I'm not proud of what I've become; not one fucking bit. In the end I may not have her, but she has helped me in more ways than she knows and I will always be thankful for that.

I owe her a lot for finally waking me up and I still think about taking my ass to Rockford and showing her how much I have changed, but I know it would be pointless. She made up her mind. I don't blame her for not wanting to give her heart to an asshole like me. I meant what I said when I told her she deserves better than me. We both knew that. That's why she left. She did what she had to do to protect her heart. She could probably see that things would turn out disastrous. She chose to stay far away from me; choosing to walk away when I couldn't.

It's a Friday night at *Walk of Shame* and I'm working the bar with Sarah. Hemy and Cale are working on training some new kid, Stone, or some shit. The kid looks like he's having a fucking blast; probably fresh out of school and dying to get his unexperienced cock wet. He's like the old version of me: dark, dirty and out for a good fuck. Well, this kid is in for the ride of his life here.

"You okay, Slade?"

I lean against the bar next to Sarah and nudge her with my shoulder. "Don't I look it," I ask teasingly. "You've been asking me that practically every fucking day. You're starting to sound like a damn broken record."

She lets out a little laugh and squeezes my arm. "It's fucking weird," she says.

"What?"

"Not having you out there. How am I supposed to get used to this shit? You not taking down every woman in your path or slamming back shots and getting naked. It's a big fucking change. Are you sure you're okay? Have you talked to-"

"Don't even bring her up, Sarah." I take a deep breath and slowly exhale. "I'm cool, okay. It's just going to take a little while to get used to the changes. You can't expect me to do this forever. I just need a change of scenery."

She nods as I walk away to help a young woman waving me over with a flirtatious smile. She's beautiful; long brown hair, big blue eyes and a body you just want to taste and fuck.

You would think she would be enough to tempt me back into my old ways, but no. Surprisingly, she does nothing for me. I'm not sure how the fuck to feel about that. All I know . . . is that I'm feeling for the first time in years. It's a scary feeling, but I think I'm going to go along for the ride; I have to.

"What can I get you," I ask while leaning over the bar.

The brunette looks at me long and hard while eyeing me up and down. She almost looks as if she's ready to strip down right here and jump my shit. She's desperate and it's actually turning me off. I kind of liked having to work for it.

"Whatever you're willing to give." She smiles before leaning in and running her tongue over her lips. "You're Slade, right? I've heard *a lot* of things about you."

I stand here slightly amused, watching as she tries desperately to make herself seem willing and available.

"I've had a rough couple days and am looking for someone to take my mind off things. I've heard you're the man to do the job." Her eyes rake over my body as she tugs on the top of her dress, exposing more of her firm breasts to me. "I've heard you're the best."

Clearing my throat, I turn my head and point across the room to Hemy. I wait for her eyes to follow. "I'm good . . . but go take your offer to my buddy over there. He'll be sure to fuck you nice and thoroughly. He'll even throw in a friend to take you up the ass while he's deep inside you, making you scream." She looks curious and a little excited. "If you're looking for a night to remember then Hemy will give you just that. He fucks like a rock star and he's dirty as shit. He'll give you anything you want. He holds nothing back in the sack."

The brunette looks me up and down before fixing the top of her dress and nodding her head. "He'll do just fine. It's a shame you're not up for the task, though. I had my tastes set on something . . . specific."

"It *is* a fucking shame." I pour her a shot of Vodka and slide it across the bar. "You're a little too late, but the shot's on me, sweetheart."

I walk away and take a deep breath; a little pissed at myself for not even being the slightest bit turned on by her offer. A couple weeks ago, I would have taken her right here in front of Sarah and then let Sarah suck her taste off my cock.

Damn. This girl really did something to me.

Sarah rushes over to me and shoves my shoulder before slapping me with a towel. "Are you serious? I would have even fucked that one. Are you sure you're not sick?"

"Sarah. Leave his ass alone."

I look up to see Cale step behind the bar, wiping down his sweaty chest with his shirt.

"How's the new kid doing?"

Cale smirks while grabbing for a bottle of water. "I'm almost positive you two fuckers are related." He opens the water and pours some over his face. "Are you sure Stone isn't your long lost fucking brother? He's a slightly smaller version of you, but with shorter hair and less tattoos. It's a little fucking scary. It's a lot like what you looked like when you were a suit."

"Good. Then he can make up for your slack like I did."

Cale punches my arm before pouring the rest of the water over his head. "She's still eating at you, isn't she?"

I ignore his question. "Have you heard from her yet?"

He shakes his head. "Nah, man. I haven't heard shit."

To be honest, I'm still a little pissed off at Cale for not telling me Aspen had a boyfriend the whole time. That asshole knew we were fucking and he couldn't even warn me? What happened to the bro code? I find that a little fucked up and he knows that.

"Dude, stop looking at me like that. I told you it wasn't my place to say shit. They were sort of on a break and plus you usually only fuck them one time and move on. I didn't know you would fall for her."

My jaw clenches from his words. I don't like hearing that shit out loud. Even though she's been on my mind constantly since she left, it really pisses me off that she has this effect on me. "Yeah, well neither did I."

"Sorry, man." Cale slaps my shoulder and starts backing away. "I'm sure she'll come back as soon as that asshole hurts her again."

The thought of that asshole even touching her makes me want to rip his fucking throat out. The thought of him hurting her, makes me want to kill him. She deserves to be treated like a fucking queen. She deserves to know that she's wanted. That's why I didn't fight harder for her to stay. I was afraid I would never be able to give her that.

Seeing the person that I've become, I have begun to believe that maybe I could have been what she needs after all. Maybe a part of me knew and I was afraid I would fall too far and then fuck up and she would leave me. If she were here now, I know I would do everything in my power to make her mine. She makes me want to be a better man; makes me want to be the old me.

Once upon a time I actually cared about my image and the way I looked from another's perspective. I would have never been caught dead working in a place like this, fucking every hot female with a wet pussy waiting between her legs and drinking myself into my grave. I actually wanted to love and to be loved. I had it before but lost it and myself, but she makes me long to be that person again. She made me realize that sometimes you have to peel back the layers to discover who someone really is. Otherwise, you may miss a remarkable person.

IT'S ALMOST CLOSING TIME AND the only ones left in the bar besides me, Cale and Sarah is a small group of females that can't keep their eyes off me or Cale. I recognize one of the girls, because I fucked her in the back a couple months ago. Her eyes haven't left me once since the crowd died down. It's starting to get a little on the creepy side.

"Dude, that chick is all up on your shit hardcore." Cale leans over the bar and starts wiping it down. "Are you sure you're not down? We can make a great fucking time out of this."

I look from Cale, over to the tatted up redhead whose eyes are practically fucking me. I'm definitely not down. I just don't feel the need. "I'm good. They're all yours, bro."

All I want to do is get my ass out of here. It's been a long ass day and I'm exhausted. The last thing I want to do is deal with some horny ass chick trying to get on my cock.

Just when I think the girls are finally going to get up and leave, I hear the door open and the sound of heels pounding on the marble flooring. The first thing I think is that another girl is joining the group of women that have been waiting impatiently for me and Cale to get off.

"We're closed," I say without looking up."

"I'm sorry. I was hoping to get here sooner."

My heart stops at the sound of her voice and my breath catches in my throat. I feel every muscle in my body tense as I bring my eyes up to see the woman that has been haunting me for the last few weeks. She's standing there in a little green dress with those sexy strappy heels that I love on her.

Holy shit, she steals my breath away.

She smiles shyly when her eyes lock with mine. She looks nervous. "I can wait outside," she says while pointing to the door. "It's not a big deal."

I get ready to respond, but Cale jumps up from the ground and hops over the bar to stop her before I can. "Holy shit! What are you doing back?"

Aspen looks at me for a second longer before turning her attention to Cale as he reaches in for a hug and shakes her back and forth. "Did you miss me that much," she asks out of breath as Cale squeezes her half to death and then releases her.

"You know it." He takes a step back and I can't help but to watch them. Everything in me wants to jump over that bar and kiss her, but I'm trying my best to hold back. "So, what the hell are you doing here? Are you staying with us again?"

My heart speeds up just at the thought of her being under the same roof as us; a chance for me to show her that I've changed; a chance to let her fall for me.

"No," she says. "I'm actually here because well . . . I moved here."

Holy fucking shit. It's suddenly hard to breathe.

"I just couldn't stay with Jay anymore. As soon as we got back home I told him it was over. I started looking around for a new job and packed up all my shit." She stops to smile at Cale. "I found a job here in a salon and decided I wanted to be back home. I've missed it here and there's nothing left for me back in Rockford. Riley is moving back in a couple months, anyway."

Cale looks paler than a fucking ghost, but I ignore his reaction and focus on Aspen. I can't help the excitement that rushes through me. Every part of me is screaming to fucking kiss her and make her mine while I can. I can't hold back. I need to do this. If I don't, someone else will.

Fuck it!

I jump over the bar, grab her face and slam my lips against hers, tasting her with desperation. The feel of her lips give me a fucking rush and I know that after this I won't be able to go on without having her as mine. I need her and I'm going to show her she needs me too.

When we're both short of breath, she pulls away and her eyes search mine. She looks scared and lost. The feeling makes my chest ache. I don't want to do that to her.

She just stares, breathing heavily, with her body trembling. Then without a word, she turns and rushes for the door. "Wait. Don't fucking run away again."

I step up behind her and grab her arm right as she's reaching for the door. She yanks it out of my grip and takes a step back as I take a step forward. It seems to be our little game. "Why? Why should I wait?"

I don't hesitate to tell her the truth this time and I don't give a shit that everyone is staring at us as if we're some kind of fucking soap opera. This time, I'm not letting her get away; I can't. "Because I love it when you touch me. It makes me feel as if I'm breathing; makes me feel . . . alive."

Her breathing picks up as I run my lips over her neck and brush her hair over her shoulder. "You make me want to be a better man. I want to take care of you. I want to make you feel wanted like you deserve." I stop to kiss her neck before gently tugging her hair to the side. "I may not be perfect all the fucking time. I'm far from it, but you make me want to be as close to it as I can be. Give me a chance to make you feel good; feel wanted. I want you to be mine. I want to be the one you snuggle with and watch a movie with at night. I want to be the one you stay home with because you don't like to go out. I don't like fucking cats, but I'll love them because you love them."

"I don't know," she whispers. "I'm scared. I can't handle being crushed by you. It will only fucking destroy me, Slade."

"I am too. Trust me. This feeling is new to me. You've done something to me and I can't stop fucking thinking about you. You've fucking ruined me. I'm not giving you up so easily."

Her lips part and it takes everything in me to not press my lips against them again and make her mine. I want her so bad, but I want her to want me just as much. I can't force her to want me this time. It will never work that way.

"You really can't stop thinking about me?" I nod my head and run my thumb over her lip. "What about all the other women, Slade? I can't be with a man like that again. I just can't." She looks around the room at the group of women watching us. She looks upset by them and a bit jealous. I don't like that look on her. "I didn't mean for my presence to distract you from your job. I just wanted to let you know you'd be seeing me around more. I didn't come looking for this."

I cup her face in my hands and step closer to her to show her I don't give a fuck about those women. "I haven't been with any other women since you. The closest I got to having sex with a woman was before you left and I was still being a horny, heartless dick. I was confused and not ready for change. I won't lie to you about that. I'll never lie to you. I haven't had sex or have even wanted to since you fucking left me that night. That's a big fucking deal for me."

A tear falls down her cheek, but she tries to hide it before I can see it. She's too late. I catch her face and rub the tear away with my thumb. She seems a bit surprised and torn. I don't blame her. I was a major dick and I don't deserve her trust. "I don't understand why, Slade. You can have anyone that you want. I do mean anyone and everyone."

"But I want you. I know I've been an asshole and I'm sorry. I don't even know how I let things go so far and let myself become an asshole . . . but when you fall it happens all too fast." I step closer to her so that my lips are brushing hers. "All I'm asking is for you to give me a chance. We can take things slow. The last thing I want to do is hurt you. I can't stop thinking about you, Aspen. No one has been able to make me feel the way you do. No one has been able to make me feel at all."

She tilts her head up and rubs her lips against mine, but doesn't kiss me. "I don't know. I'm not sure it's a good idea."

"How do you feel about me?" I tilt her face up so she can look me in the eyes. The eyes always give the heart away. "Tell me how you feel. I don't want a bullshit answer this time. I'm standing here in front of everyone asking you if you feel the same way I do. Tell me the truth."

Her eyes search mine and I can see her walls break down a bit. She cares for me, but just how much? Is it enough? I can only hope. "I haven't stopped thinking about you since the first time I laid eyes on you. I knew then that I wouldn't be able to forget you. I was right. I was hoping that I'd be able to go the whole week and force myself to hate you. It didn't happen. Every day, I fell further for you." She reaches up and wraps her hands in my hair and gently tugs on it. "Then you opened up to me and I fell even more. It was unstoppable and I knew I was screwed in the best way possible. I wanted to know more. I wanted to help ease your pain. I wanted to cure you."

I pull her face to mine and suck in her bottom lip before releasing it. "You did fucking cure me. Now give me a chance to cure you. If I fuck up you can punish me." I smirk and she lightly taps my cheek. "I mean it."

Her eyes search mine for a second and I leave them open for her. I want her to read them; to see how I truly feel and that I meant every word that I said. "We'll take things slow," she asks. "At my pace?"

"At your pace." I smile as I bite her lip and press my body against hers. "Except for in the bedroom."

She laughs and again, it's the most beautiful sound in the fucking world. Especially when it's because of me. I never want to forget that sound. "I think I can handle that," she whispers. "Just don't hurt me, please. I can't handle it."

"I won't do that. If I hurt you I will only be hurting myself more." I gently suck her bottom lip into my mouth before kissing her. She kisses me back with a desperation that says she's missed me as much as I've missed her before pulling away and placing her forehead to mine.

"Maybe you should stay at my house tonight. You know, come help me unpack."

"All right, guys," Cale jumps in between us and places his hand on my chest. "This is getting too fucking mushy. Slade, are you running a fucking fever?"

"Fuck you, Cale." I push him out of the way and grab my woman, throwing her over my shoulder. She giggles and slaps my ass. I like it. "Have fun closing up the bar. I'm fucking out."

Before Cale or Sarah can respond, I'm out the fucking door. I smack Aspen's perfect little ass, causing her to bite me as I head for the white Jeep that she points to.

Looks like I have a lot to prove before Aspen will completely trust me and give herself to me fully. I'm willing to give it my all. She deserves better than what she's had and that's what I'll be working to be. She's opened my eyes and I'm not going to fucking let them close again. I'm tired of not living and just getting by day by day, trying my best to feel less dead.

I have no idea where this will take me and if it will work out, but it's worth fighting for. That's the only thing I know at the moment.

I'm going to show this woman that I can be her man and more; show her and myself that I'm still human . . .

The End of #1

Missing Slade and Aspen already? Be sure to check out the rest of the Walk Of Shame series to get updates on where they stand. This is the order of the series. Also, be sure to check out Hemy's blurb to see what his story is about. Don't miss out. Thank you!

Slade (Walk Of Shame #1)
Hemy (Walk Of Shame #2)
Cale (Walk Of Shame #3)

HEMY
WALK OF SHAME #2
AVAILABLE NOW

My name is Hemy Knox and I'm a fucking heartbreaker . . .

I've hurt the one person that means the most to me in life; the only woman I have ever fucking loved. I let the drugs, alcohol and wild life take over; consume me. I got her where I wanted her and ripped her fucking heart out.

Since then, I've spent countless nights having dirty, meaningless sex with a multitude of people; only leaving them wanting and begging for more with no regrets. Some may even call me the devil; soulless.

They look and judge, but there is one thing they don't know; no one does. I want more than this life of stripping and sleeping around; the never ending party. I want love and everything that comes with it; that high that never ends. The problem is . . . I only want it with her.

Onyx.

She refuses to be mine . . . again. She's smart and it's a mother fucking pain in my ass; guarding her heart while ripping mine right out of my fucking chest. I can't say that I blame her. I always was a dumb ass when it came to the emotions of a woman, especially her.

She wants to see me suffer as much as I made her; watch me wither and fucking die at her feet. She wants to crush me until I'm no longer breathing and I will let her, because it hurts far less than not having her as mine.

I will stop at nothing to make her mine again. The pain only drives me harder; feeding my fury and giving me a reason to live . . . her.

Author's note Due to strong language and a very high amount of sexual content, this book is not intended for readers under the age of 18. This is #2 in the Walk Of Shame series of novellas that will all be STANDALONE reads. This includes F/M and F/M/M so if you're not into dirty sex scenes with filthy language, then this book is not for you. If you are . . . then, come meet the dirty boys of Walk Of Shame.

ACKNOWLEDGEMENTS

FIRST AND FOREMOST, I'D LIKE to say a big thank you to all my loyal readers that have given me support over the last couple years and have encouraged me to continue with my writing. Your words have all inspired me to do what I enjoy and love. Each and every one of you mean a lot to me and I wouldn't be where I am if it weren't for your support and kind words.

I'd also like to thank my special friend, Author of Accepted Fate and editor, Charisse Spiers. She has put a lot of time into helping me put this story together and through this, we have become very close friends. I'm lucky to have her be a part of this journey with me. Please everyone look out for her debut novel Accepted Fate and her upcoming release for July 3rd, Twisting Fate. She has shown me so much support through this whole process and it would be nice to be able to return the favor. Her story is beautifully written and something that the world shouldn't miss out on.

Also, all of my beta readers, both family and friends that have taken the time to read my book and give me pointers throughout this process. My friend Charisse Spiers, Hetty Whitmore Rasmussen and my friend and blogger Rebecca Pugh from *Becca's Books*. You guys have helped encourage me more than you know. *Bestsellers and Beststellars of Romance* for hosting my cover reveal, blog tour and release day blitz. Hetty has been a big part in making this happen. You all have. Thank you all so much.

I'd like to thank another friend of mine, Clarise Tan from *CT Cover Creations* for creating my cover. You've been wonderful to work with and have helped me in so many ways.

Thank you to my boyfriend, friends and family for understanding my busy schedule and being there to support me through the hardest part. I know it's hard on everyone, and everyone's support means the world to me.

Last but not least, I'd like to thank all of the wonderful book bloggers that have taken the time to support my book and help spread the word. You all do so much for us authors and it is greatly appreciated. I have met so many friends on the way and you guys are never forgotten. You guys rock. Thank you!

ABOUT THE AUTHOR

VICTORIA ASHLEY GREW UP IN Rockford, IL and has had a passion for reading for as long as she can remember. After finding a reading app where it allowed readers to upload their own stories, she gave it a shot and writing became her passion.

She lives for a good romance book with tattooed bad boys that are just highly misunderstood and is not afraid to be caught crying during a good read. When she's not reading or writing about bad boys, you can find her watching her favorite shows such as Sons Of Anarchy, Dexter and True Blood.

She is the author of Wake Up Call and This Regret and is currently working on more works for 2014.

Contact her at:

Facebook:
Victoria Ashley Author and Victoria Ashley-Author

Goodreads:
Victoria Ashley or Slade (Walk Of Shame #1)

Or you can follow Walk Of Shame's Facebook page for more info on the upcoming releases.
Find her other books on Amazon as well.

Other Books by Victoria Ashley

Wake Up Call
This Regret

Walk of Shame
Slade (Walk Of Shame #1)

24917517R00106

Made in the USA
San Bernardino, CA
10 October 2015